Keegan

FOSTER'S PRIDE BOOK 5

KATHI S. BARTON

World Castle Publishing, LLC
Pensacola, Florida
Copyright © Kathi S. Barton 2022
Hardcover ISBN: 9798846302204
Paperback ISBN: 9781958336625
eBook ISBN: 9781958336632
First Edition World Castle Publishing, LLC, August 15, 2022
http://www.worldcastlepublishing.com
Licensing Notes
Cover: Karen Fuller
Editor: Maxine Bringenberg

Prologue

Keegan closed up the books he'd been working on and put them in the safe behind him. Tomorrow he was going to be moving everything into his new domain, and he'd feel better about the bigger safe as well as the good locks on the doors. Just as he was coming out of the building he'd been using as a temporary place, he was knocked on his ass. He ended up falling backwards and hitting his head on the cornerstone.

He must have been out for only a few seconds when someone was jerking him up from the ground. Still dizzy, Keegan couldn't focus on the man holding him, but he could smell that he was a bear. The hard shake to his body had him lashing out with his fist, and for the second time, he was down. This time, however, so was the man.

"I asked you a fucking question. Where the fuck is he?" Keegan said he didn't know what he was talking about. "Oh, you don't, do you? Well, who the hell knocked you back with tiny little feet like that?"

The snow was covered in little footprints. However, there were a great many of them that weren't so tiny. Looking up at the man when he stood up, Keegan let a little of his lion go so he'd be healed a little. Standing up, not feeling so bad now that he had done that, he asked the man what the hell he was going on about.

"The kid. Where is he? You have to have seen him. Or are you one of those evangelistic people?" Keegan asked him what the hell that was supposed to mean. "You know, those religious shits that would rather die than to give up on someone."

"That's not what that word means. And what the hell would I have to give up on someone? Unless it's you. Then I'd gladly let the police handle this." He reached for his brother, knowing that Cass had been on his way to meet him here today. Keegan told him what was going on and that he might need the police. "I don't know anything about a kid. However, I do know you're going to be in trouble for knocking me down and making my head hurt if you don't get out of my face."

"Sure. Like I'm worried about you." The man released his bear enough that Keegan could see he was a brown bear, and wasn't in good shape. When a shifter didn't allow their other half out once in a while, things could get nasty. "So you see, you're going to tell me what happened to the kid. He stole some fruit from my store."

"He must be desperate then. I've been by your store, Hank, and there isn't usually anything I'd eat there." He drew back his fist, and Keegan braced himself for the blow. But when nothing happened, he opened one eye to peer at the man. "Ronan? I didn't know you were in town."

"Cass and I were going to surprise you by having dinner with you. Our wives are out shopping. This man bothering you, little brother?" He didn't normally care for being referred to as little anything, but he thought Ronan was making it clear to Hank that he was the brother of the king of lions. "I can dispatch him now if you wish. I know his sleuth is looking for him too. Seems he's been taking money from the coffers at the bruin."

"Sounds like something he'd be doing. He said he was looking for a kid. I haven't any idea because as soon as I came out of the building here, I was thrown to the ground. He said the kid did it, but I think Hank did it for shits and giggles." Hank said it was the kid. "I've not seen one. He pointed out that there are footprints, but I'm thinking these could have been made at any time by anyone."

That was when he saw the kid across the street from them watching things going on. However, Keegan didn't think it was a kid but a girl. And she looked beaten to shit too. Telling his brother, Ronan told him that Cass was on the case. Since he didn't have the head right now for figuring out what that meant, he sat down in the snow again and pulled a ball of the fluffy white stuff to his aching head.

In less time than it would have taken him to walk home, six blocks from there, not only was the sleuth with them but Hank was being arrested for assault and battery. Cass had been with the girl for the last ten minutes, and it looked as if they were getting along fine. When the ambulance pulled up, Cass pushed him out of the way and put the girl in it. With a wink, Cass told him he could heal himself.

Standing now, the snow coming down once again, he let it fall over his face. There were things going on around him, but he really did have a headache from hell. Almost as soon as he decided he couldn't stand much longer, he found himself in bed, at his home, with a compress on his head. Parker and his mom were standing over him.

"I'm going to be sick." As soon as he said it, Parker touched his head. Not only was he no longer ill, but his pain was gone as well. "What happened that I ended up here?"

"Ronan said you looked like you needed some assistance. So I popped in and popped you here. Hank is in serious trouble, and the woman is being treated for her wounds." Keegan asked her what lady. "The woman that Hank beat up that was going through his trash. Not a kid, as Hank thought, but a full-grown undernourished woman. She's going to be fine."

"Why do I feel like I've fallen through the rabbit hole here?" His mom laughed and handed him a glass of juice. "Mom, please tell me what's going on. I'm a sick boy."

"You're no more sick than I am. A woman was going through Hank's trash to get herself something to eat. He caught her, thinking she was a boy and beat her up for what she'd been doing. Once she was able to escape, she zoomed by you and knocked you on your bottom. She's the one that called Ronan to come to help you." He asked if she was a lion too. "Honey, she's a lioness. And yes, she is. Very nice girl too, if you ask me."

He didn't but kept that to himself. As he laid there, thinking how much better he was feeling, he closed his eyes. Whatever came from this, Keegan had a feeling he was going to be having a mate, as well as someone gunning for him. Christ, why couldn't things just be normal? He supposed that was a question for the fates. Closing his eyes, he let himself go to sleep. It was going to be a long day tomorrow, what with moving and getting himself set up.

Chapter 1

"Where do you want this?" Keegan looked at his brother Loman and asked him what it said on the box. "I'm not sure. This side says kitchen. The one facing you says bathroom, and there is a sticky note—now that I think about it is more than likely your note—says it goes in the front office."

"Yes, they all have sticky notes on them. And if the notes fall off, I've written down under it where it goes. Didn't we go over this when we were at the temporary office? Twice?" Loman acted like he was going to toss the box at him but laughed. "You've no idea how much I appreciate your help on this. I've been here for three days, and I don't feel any closer to having things set up yet. The others said they'd be by later, but I hate leaving things to the last second."

"Because you're OCD. I always knew that you were obsessive-compulsive, Keegan, but I never realized how much you are—hey, why did your room when we were growing up always look like a thunderstorm went through it?" Keegan told him. "Oh. I guess I am a bit of a slob. Do you suppose my mate will be too? I mean, we're supposed to be alike, right?"

"No, you're supposed to complement one another. I pity the woman that comes into your home and finds it like you left our room all the time." He shivered. "Mom said there were socks under your bed that had been there since high school. Damn, Loman, you've been out of school since...I don't know? Ten years?"

"About that. However, what she didn't tell anyone was that they were brand new socks that were still in the bag." Keegan nodded, not believing a word about it. "Ask mom."

"Ask mom what? Are you two fighting again? My goodness, sons, you're grown men. Stop picking at each other." Mom gave him a hug and a kiss and then walked over to Loman. "They were new socks, Loman. However, the story is funnier if I don't mention that part. Are you two hungry? How about you take your poor neglected mother out to lunch? Also, I have to run some things by the hospital, and I'd like a ride there. That poor woman. To have been out like she was on her own with no food for that long...well, let's have some lunch."

Keegan wasn't going to ask about the woman that was still in the hospital. She'd been found three nights ago after knocking him on his ass. Then, if that wasn't bad enough, he'd been hit by Hank, a bear shifter that had a 'fresh' marketplace in the area because the woman had been stealing from his dumpster. Since he'd been busy packing and then unpacking for his new office, no one had asked him to go to the hospital to find out if he belonged to her.

Not that he wasn't excited to have a mate. He'd seen how much his brothers were in love with theirs. However, he had more than enough on his plate at the moment, and he didn't want to have to divide his time between her and the office being set up. Working at getting this place finished so that he'd be able to devote all his time—

"*That is perhaps the lamest thing I've ever heard one of you guys thinking about. What if you...? Never mind. You're an idiot.*" He hid a smile when Parker spoke to him. "*I have to get my life set up so that it is perfect before I want to find my other half.*" She was mocking him. He just knew it.

"*You have to admit, I have a lot going on right now. I've been keeping my head to the grindstone for a few months now, and I want to stretch my wings out and have some fun when it's done.*" She told him he was an idiot again. "*Why? Because I don't conform to things like you want me to? Come on, Parker. You know as well as I do that whatever happens, and she is my mate, there is going to be trouble from something that she has going on. Baggage. Then there is the fact that she's going to be coming to me with a lot of wounds that are going to make it so —*"

"*Shut the fuck up.*" He had to laugh. Telling her he was joking didn't buy him any brownie points with her, either. "*She has a lot of baggage, as you said. But I think that this is far worse than any of the rest of us had, Keegan. She's healed for the most part. And like the others, I'm assuming it's because you have had contact with her. Minimal, yes, but you did have some. She's not*

Loman's mate, either. He's been by."

He felt bad because he could have gone there and healed her completely if he'd not been being an ass. Telling her that he'd come up with his mom when she came by, Parker thanked him. Then he asked her what had been on his mind since the night that she'd knocked him down.

"What are her troubles, Parker? I'm sure you know what some of them are and are working on them as we speak." She told him that she'd not done anything to help her as yet as there wasn't enough information that she could find. *"I don't understand. Are you saying that she can block you?"*

"Yes." He laughed. The frustration in her voice had him laughing again. He told his mom what was going on and how he was going to go with her to the hospital. *"Do you have any idea how much I hate the idea that I can't get into her head? Let me tell you, too, I've tried. But I have a feeling that she'll hurt me if I try too hard."*

"Don't hurt her." He felt his cat run along his skin when he thought of her, a near stranger being hurt. *"I'm going to make my way over there now. If she's hurting, I'm going to heal her. Then we'll talk about*

anything else she has going on in her life. I don't mind there being a great deal, but since I'm working for the family now, I'm going to need some major help setting up things to make it work for all of us." She told him she'd do it if he had ten minutes to tell her where things went. He liked that idea even better.

It didn't take him long to get some lunch for the others and head to the hospital. His mom told him how many people had been in the room when she'd left the room to get food. Keegan got that many salads and sandwiches. Just as they were getting on the elevator, his mom took a phone call, and he waited on her. Since he had no idea where he'd been headed, sitting in one of the chairs to wait on her seemed the best move. When she put her phone away, she came toward him. He could see that she was upset about whatever had transpired on the phone.

"I have to go. One of the ladies in our sewing group has just lost her husband. I need to go be with her." Keegan told her to go and hugged her. "Oh, the room number. You'll need that."

After he had the information that he needed, he got into the elevator and made his way up to the sixth floor. Whatever happened now was going to be up to him to make sure that the woman was safe. Or do whatever she needed to help her.

"Hello." He looked up at the woman coming towards him with an IV pole. "You must be Keegan. Your family has talked about nothing but you since I woke up in here. If you don't mind, I have to walk a little more. To get my blood flowing, they told me. That food, I'm hoping you have enough to share, smells heavenly."

"Yes, I'm Keegan." She nodded but didn't say what her name was. "My mom had to go to one of her friends. Her husband had just passed. Are the rest of my family in your room?"

"No. They left. Not because they wanted to, but I'd had enough of them hovering over me all the time. They're very vocal about shit, aren't they? And that Parker? Well, she's pushy. All of them are, but she's particularly pushy." He agreed with her. "My name is Kerri Terrell. I'm twenty-five. I had a job up until six months ago. A home as well as a nice car. Then, my mother came along with her new boyfriend, someone about my age and decided that I was unfit to be a mom and took my daughter from me as well. I can't work because of this shit hanging over me. I haven't any place to live. No money that I can get to, nor do I have the first clue at how to get it all back from them. I thought that I'd get that all out there at one time and let you mull it over while I have something to eat. I'm starving."

"Wow, that's a lot at the first meeting, don't you think? Not that I mind. I know that Parker will be jealous of how much more that I know than she does." Kerry smiled at him and told him that was the point. "Thanks. It's not often that I can get one up on my sisters-in-laws. I'm your mate, by the way. As I'm also sure you know, I'm a lion. Mom told me that you were a lioness."

"I am. To both. Your mate and a lioness. I don't think anyone has ever called me a lioness before. But it does have a nice ring to it, doesn't it? Anyway, I'm not sure where to go from here. I know about mates and such. My mother is a world-class bitch of a lioness." He asked her about her daughter as they entered her room. "She's beautiful. Her name is Allyson, and she's eight. I had her too young, and my mother is holding that against me as I made her a grandmother at such a young age. I don't know why she thinks anyone would care. She rarely had anything to do with Allyson before she took her from me."

"Did she have a good reason for taking her? And where is Allyson's father? I'm assuming that he's a lion too." She looked so sad for a moment, then smiled at him. "You're very beautiful, Kerri. If your daughter is half as beautiful as you are, I'm going to bar her from ever dating."

"She would tell you that men are sucky anyway. Right now, I'm happy for her not being aware of them. Her father is dead. His name was Farley Smithy. We weren't mates. I don't know how it is that I was able to conceive his child, but I don't know a great many things about my life as my mother, she again lied about every little thing that was asked of her. Mother told me that I wasn't to look into things as I might find things that I don't want to. I didn't. Just to keep the peace with her. My dad, he's gone too. Suicide. I was told that he murdered Farley when he found out I was pregnant with his child at seventeen. Then he killed himself. The thing is, my dad didn't seem to be upset with my having Allyson, nor did he seem to dislike Farley in any way. They got along great, I assumed. And why did it take him eight years to get upset with Farley about me having a child? My mom, Belinda, thinks my dad was too old for her anyway. I haven't any idea how she came up with that idea as she was two years older than him. But they're both gone now, and I'm missing them so much. Farley was a good dad to his daughter. Dad loved her too."

Keegan was going to need a pad of paper to keep up with the things she was telling him. While he initially thought he'd have to pry things from her to get to the bottom of things, she was volunteering the information like she'd been just waiting for him to come along so she could tell him. When she smiled at him, he couldn't help it. He smiled back.

"It's too much, right?" He laughed while nodding. Keegan opened the sub wrapper up and put it in front of her. "I haven't any idea why I'm so talkative right now. Usually, I'm not. I mean, I don't say a word until I have thought it through over and over again and have it set in my head. But I feel like if I can get this all out, telling you what my life is about right now, you'll either run to the hills or help me. I'm hoping that you'll help me. Allyson is all I have in the world. And to be perfectly honest with you, Keegan, I don't think my dad killed himself. Nor do

I think that Farley was killed by him. I think that my mom did it or her boytoy, Franklin."

When she burst into tears, he moved the little table out of the way and held her. Picking her up off the bed, he pulled her into his lap so that he could get her closer to him. Her lioness purred, and his did as well. He didn't know if he really was hearing her cat or not, but he was positive that it was something along those lines.

When she stopped crying, he continued to hold her. Telling her things about himself that he'd not shared with anyone before. His family might know some of the things he was talking about but not the detail that he was giving to Kerri. Looking up at him, he saw she had one blue eye and one brown. He thought it was the most beautiful thing he'd ever seen.

"Where does your mother live?" She asked him what he was going to do. "Get my daughter back from her. Also, I'll have my family look into things deeper for you. There has to be something going on that she was able to separate the two of you. I can't believe that you were unfit to raise her. Not after eight years of you having her."

They talked the entire time they were eating. There was plenty of food left over, and he handed it off to the nursing station to share. Keegan was glad to see that Kerri was feeling better now that she had eaten. He did as well. There was no stress now. He didn't even feel the need to get to his office and finish it up.

He reached out to Rogue first when they were finished eating. She had connections with the Feds that might be able to look into things that no one else could. After telling her what he had in the way of information, he contacted Parker. She told him that she would find out what she could from the earth about the death of Farley and George.

"She has a daughter? Your family will be thrilled. Let me see what I can find out about how she's doing." He told Kerri what Parker was doing, and he was glad now that he'd come to the hospital. *"Can you leave there? With Kerri? Like now?"*

"What's going on, Parker?" She told him as best she could while remaining calm. He looked at Kerri. "Your daughter is in the ER right now. She has been hurt. Parker said she's not sure how badly she is hurt as there seems to be old wounds with the new ones.

We'll go down there now and see if we can talk to her."

They were headed to the elevator when Parker popped into the hallway with them. Touching Kerri, she told her how she could dress herself now and to make herself look very professional as well as she was now an immortal.

"You need to know that now." Kerri asked her why. "I'm not as good at seeing into the future as Sarah is, but she wanted me to tell you that so that you'd not shield away from whatever happens. In other words, I think she wants you to be yourself. Again, I don't know the particulars, but she wanted to make sure you knew that before facing what is going on in the ER department."

As soon as they were off the elevator, he could hear a commotion. While he wasn't sure that it was his daughter that was crying, he made his way right to the room where the cries were coming from. Entering the room, he told Ronan that he was going to need him here right now. He was thrilled to death when Ronan popped magically into the hall behind him with his brother, Don. Don had brought him here with the same magic that Parker used to do the same thing. It was very helpful when they did stuff like that.

~*~

Ronan entering the room, had everyone stop talking and yelling and to drop to the floor. He might have been impressed with how quickly they had done it if not for the child lying on the gurney bleeding from a nasty head wound. Going to her first, he only touched his finger to the wound to have it heal. She looked up at him and smiled. Ronan couldn't help but to smile back at her. Christ, she was as pretty as her mother was.

"They're trying to get me to lie for them." He asked her who that might be. "That man over there. I am not going to call him daddy no matter how much that person there beats me." She looked around Ronan then. "Mom? Mom, is that really you?"

The union was very telling. The two of them hugged each other like it had been forever since they'd seen one another. When he stepped back to allow Keegan to go to the two of them, he turned to the others in the room. The older woman, who said her name was Belinda, told him that she was Allyson's mother.

"Really? Well, I don't believe you. Do you have any idea what the penalty is for lying to your king? You'll tell me the truth, or so help me, I'll take you to task. And I'm in no mood to be kind about it, either. I was enjoying a nice afternoon with my own children and had to come here to straighten you out. Are you the child's mother or not?" She fought against it. Blood began to stream down her chin when she bit into her lips. "Tell me now."

"She's not my daughter. But that gives you no right to do anything about the situation. You should mind your own fucking business. My daughter has been taking her round everywhere, telling people that she's my granddaughter, and I won't allow that. It makes me look older than I really am." He asked her how old she was. "That is none of your business."

"She's sixty-six. Two years older than my grandfather was. At least he didn't care that I was his grandchild." Belinda told the little girl to shut her fucking mouth. "Why? So you can lie some more? I'm not going to be your little girl. I'm not going to call that idiot over there my dad or you mom either. I don't like either of you. He's stupid if you ask me to even want to have a thing to do with your old wrinkly body. Gross."

Ronan had to fight hard to hold in his laughter. He loved this kid. She simply told it like it was. When he asked her how she'd come to be with her grandmother, it was Kerri that answered him. The two of them were like two peas in a pod when she looked as if she was going to lose her shit at his question.

"She, my mother, stole my child from me and anything else she could get her hands on. I was away on a business trip when I got news from the police in town that my home had been burnt to the ground. Before I could even think about all the things that Allyson and I lost, I was also told that my daughter had been taken into the care of my mother. For neglect. Allyson was at a camp for the week I was gone, and she went there and took her from their care. Lying by telling them that I had died. Do you believe that shit?" Kerri got into his face, and he backed away from her. She was a tiny little thing, but she looked like she could take him on and win. "When I returned home, imagine my surprise and hurt when I found out that my mother had filed a report against me about not only being a bad parent to my child, but she was telling people that I burned my own home down to get attention. That would be her modest operandum, not mine. After that, everything went to shit. I lost my job, everything that I owned and my mother, dearest mother, had my accounts sealed so that I couldn't touch them. Claiming that I'd gotten the money by selling drugs and other women."

Ronan looked at Keegan, who was smiling at him. Asking him if he had anything to add, his brother said that he thought that his mate was doing a fine job so far. Ronan had to admit that she was doing a good job of telling him what was going on. However, he wasn't the bad guy in all of this. But he did call the police in.

When the police arrived, there was a lot more shouting and screaming going on. Kerri's mother and boytoy, a name that he thought suited the much younger man, were saying that it was all Kerri's fault for being a terrible mother to her little girl. That was the reason that they'd had to step in and take her from her. Ronan was glad to see that Keegan had slipped out of the room with Allyson. It wasn't right that she had to witness this shit. Ronan put his fingers in his mouth and whistled. The room became dead quiet.

"This is how this is going to work. You're going to keep your mouths shut until you're asked a — did anyone ask you a question, Mrs. Terrell? No, they did not. Shut the hell up until someone asks you for something." Ronan was getting frustrated, too, and he wasn't even involved in all this drama other than he was their king. He turned to Officer Donley and told him, in as brief of details as he could, what was going on. "The woman over there is Belinda Terrell, mother-in-law to my brother Keegan. The man, I don't know his name but is being called boytoy."

Donley burst out laughing when Belinda told him that he was her fiancé. "His name is Roger Lipscomb. He and I are set to be married in a few weeks. And I'd appreciate it if you were to not make judgements on us. He and I are in love, and once we're married, we're going to adopt Allyson and raise her as our daughter."

The man, Roger, looked terrified in that moment, and Ronan had a feeling that not only was he surprised by the upcoming nuptials, but also, he was having second thoughts about being with Belinda.

Slipping out of the room to find his brother,

he wasn't surprised that Kerri had come along with him. Talking to her as he sniffed out his brother, she told him that she wasn't going to allow anyone to take her daughter from her.

"I don't want that either." She looked at him oddly, and he asked her what was going on. Instead of answering him, she stepped into the elevator and said she was going to the cafeteria. That she'd meet him there. Getting into the opening before it closed, he wasn't sure if he should be pissed or not when she told him he wasn't welcome. Ending up in the dining area, he sat down with Keegan as he was enjoying a piece of pie with Allyson. "Can you please tell me what the hell is going on here? I thought that it was a simple thing between a mother and daughter. But this is far beyond anything that I can figure out."

"I don't know yet." Ronan then asked him if he knew what was going to happen now. "Nope. I'm enjoying talking to my soon-to-be daughter. Kerri told me everything going on when I got to her room. Which is a great deal. Not even counting this thing with her mother. Parker is the one that told me that Allyson was in the ER. We got there about the same time you did. Other than a few details that really aren't relevant to any of that going on, I don't have a clue. Brook is looking into things for me as to what happened to the report that was filed and into why they were given Allyson to stay with them. Also, and this is something that I've only just thought of again, Kerri thinks that her mom killed her father as well as Allyson's biological father."

"I can answer that one. At least I have an idea of what happened. It's something that she does." Keegan was already besotted by his mate. Smiling at her when she handed him another slice of pie, Ronan took the one that she offered him without complaint. "She bribed them. I'm not sure how but that's what she does when things don't go her way. Like she bribed the principal at my high school, trying to get me banned from my graduation. I was about six months along with Allyson when she did that."

"Did it work?" Kerri shook her head and told him what the man had done. "Good for him. But I don't think that she learned her lesson about not being able to bribe people when it's against the law. What other things has she done in the name of— is she really taking Allyson from you because she doesn't want anyone to know that she's a grandma?"

"Yes, that sounds like something she'd do. Up until I was old enough to understand what she was doing to me, she used to buy me clothing that was way too young for me. She dressed me as a kid that was ten or so years younger than I was at the time. Then when I started to show that I was having my daughter, I was hidden away. I was glad that I turned eighteen before Allyson was born, or she would have made me give her up for adoption. In fact, she had the couple lined up that was going to take her from me, and it all arranged for me to be put in a place where I'd never get out. Mother claimed that I was insane and that I'd harm myself and the child if someone didn't take me in hand. She told people that I was suicidal as well. I think too that she killed my father and Allyson's father to get them out of her way."

"She's a nutball." Kerri scolded her daughter about using that term. "Well, she is. When she took me out of camp the day that my mom left, she locked me in a cage until she had no choice but to let me go. I think that the neighbors complained about me screaming. I screamed day and night until I was sick from it. I got this knot on my head this morning because I wouldn't call boytoy daddy when he dropped me off at the doctor's. She hit me with a book that he was reading. She wouldn't let me see my mom, telling me that she had forsaken me and didn't want me anymore."

"You didn't believe her, I take it." Ronan was given a glare like his own wife had given him on occasion. Reaching out to his family, he asked for some help. *"I'm in over my head here. This is more than…I can't believe the things that are going on, and Keegan is just sitting here like he hasn't a care in the world."*

"I would say that he feels as if he doesn't. His big brother is there helping him. He's found his mate, and he has a daughter." He told his mom that she was a pretty little thing too. *"I just bet she is. Mouthy, too, I'm thinking. I'm on my way there. Also, you should tell them that the police have gone to the house where Allyson was being held captive in. You're not going to believe the things the girls found when they took a peek around."*

He'd believe just about anything right now. When his family started showing up, he felt like he had a better handle on the situation. There was safety in numbers. He was talking a great deal to Kerri and Allyson, getting information that he could use if it came to him having to exact payment from the people that had decided that their way was better than the police wanted things done. Stupid woman. She was going to be in big trouble if she didn't calm her noodle down.

Parker and his mom showed up first. Mom handed a bag to Allyson, telling her that it was clothing that she could wear home. When Allyson asked her where she was going, mom told her with Keegan and her mother. That seemed to make the child happy, and when she darted off with her mom to change, he looked at his brother.

"What do you see happening with this? I mean, I can take Kerri's mother to task for lying to me, but as for the rest, that's human things that I have no control over." Keegan asked about the kidnapping of Allyson from the camp. "Without proof, I can't do a thing about that either. I'm sorry. But again, I think this would fall under the police. Kidnapping is something that I can charge her with. But think we should let the police handle that. Until it gets out of hand. Then I'll take over."

"There was a restraining order against the mother to stay five feet from Kerri and her daughter.

She did break that law. I know that's a human thing too, but I'm thinking that once you see the shit at the house, you'll be able to step in and take over." He thanked Parker for that. "No worries about that. However, Belinda has left the hospital. The police told her not to leave town. I don't think she will simply because she has it in her head to take Allyson by any means possible. Boytoy has left too, but he didn't go with Belinda. I think she terrified him a little when she mentioned marriage."

When Kerri and Allyson came back, he was surprised to see that Allyson had been crying. When he looked at Keegan, he just shook his head. He was willing to let it go if Keegan was going to take care of it. However, he'd fallen for the little girl, and he didn't want her upset. Her mom, either. Kerri asked if she could say something. They all agreed that she could anytime she wanted.

"I'd like to go home. I'm not sure where that would be, but I'm assuming that Keegan has one to shelter us in." Keegan said that he did indeed have them a home they could stay in. "Thank you for that. I have a grandfather out there someplace, too, that I'd like to have here with me. He won't have to live in the house with us, but I miss him too. He's my father's dad. Grandda has been hidden away from me since before I had Allyson. Dad thought that mom would use him to get my dad to do her deeds. He never told me what they were, but I'm assuming more of the same. I miss them both."

"Your mothers doing?" She told Keegan that her dad had hidden him away so that Belinda couldn't hurt him. "He's welcome to live anywhere I have a place. I'd love to have him around if you don't mind."

"No. I'd like that too. Please." Kerri looked at her daughter before speaking again. Ronan braced himself for whatever came out next. He thought that this so far had been a hell of a day, and he had a feeling that they weren't even scratching the surface of things. "I don't know now what I'm supposed to do. I know that this is a great deal to spring on all of you, and if not for Keegan, well, I don't know what I might have done. I'm getting…I was getting to the point where I was ready to just end it all. You've no idea what I've gone through in the last year, and I'm so very grateful for anything and everything that you can do to help us."

"We're here for you. You're my family now. All of our family and we take care of our own. You just let us help, and you'll see that we're true to our words. We'll keep you and Allyson safe." She thanked Keegan then the rest of them. When he stood up, his body stiff with anger, the others stood as well. It wasn't until Keegan pushed both his mate and daughter behind him that Ronan stood up.

"There you are. You're coming home with me now." Keegan asked Belinda how she thought that was going to work. "There are police all around my home, and I'm going to take Allyson there to explain things to them. I hate that you people are keeping me from her. I told you that I'm going to adopt her. The police have it in their head that she's been held captive by me. Come on, Allyson, darling. We'll get this all cleared up in no time."

"Nope. I'm not going anywhere with you. You're insane. I told you this before, but apparently, you didn't listen. You're not my mom. You're not going to hold me in that cage anymore. And I'm going to do what I want." The kid shifted from her human self to a lion in seconds. The roar that she gave her grandmother was impressive in that it made her point to the older woman. Chasing her grandmother out of the dining room, he looked at his brother.

"You're in big trouble. I hope you're aware of that." Keegan grinned and told him that he thought it was wonderful. "I'm glad to hear you say that. However, you should know that it's not going to end well for Belinda."

"I didn't think it would." He looked in the direction that Allyson had gone. "I wonder if Belinda remembers that she's a cat too. I think I would have wet myself had she been after me."

They were all laughing when they found Allyson. She was her other half, dressed in a pair of warm pants and a jacket. Asking if they could go home, he said it was fine by him. But he did want to have them all over for dinner tonight.

"Tomorrow night? Please?" He nodded at his brother when he asked. "I have a lot of things to take care of at home. And I left my office about half finished to come here. I'm not unhappy that I came. I'm thrilled, but we have a lot of things to talk about. And I need to get all this settled in my mind."

"I'm right there with you. I think having it all at once is something that I've never had before. Like you, I'm happy that she's here and that you're able to keep her safe, but it's a lot." They both hugged each other and then parted ways. When they were walking away from him, he thought about how wonderful they looked as a family. It made him want to go home and hug his own little family.

Heading home, he stopped by the market and picked up a dozen pink roses for Brook. Then he got a rose each to add to her flowers for his daughters. Ronan loved being a dad and to have a mate that took such care of him and their family.

Chapter 2

Her home was a mess, and Belinda hated it. The police and the fucking Feds had been tearing things up since before she had arrived here the first time. She had thought that going back to make Allyson tell them that she'd been treated well here would help, but the kid had actually chased her out of the hospital as her cat. Damn kid. Belinda wasn't happy about any of the things going on right now. Even the cabinets in the kitchen had been emptied, and her lovely dishes were broken on the floor. Asking the Federal man, she wouldn't commit his name to her memory as she didn't think he deserved it if they were going to replace her things.

"No." She told him if he were to tell her what they were looking for, she could save them some time. "We found what we came here to find. Now we're just looking around. You should also know that we've confiscated the cage in the basement. As well as the things, pitiful amount there is, in the room that smelled like Allyson. How could you do that to your own flesh and blood is beyond me, but the Feds are involved now, and you'll be charged if we find a single spot of DNA in that cage that belongs to Allyson. Understand?"

She simply walked away from him. Pulling out her cell phone, she looked for her attorney's name so she could call him. While she'd not used him herself, she knew that her husband had. It was the same attorney she'd been hounding for the last few months to get the will read so she could get on with her life. When someone answered, she asked to speak to the attorney that was in charge of her estate.

"You'll have to give me a bit more information than that, I'm afraid. What are your name and date of birth, and I'll look at what you might be talking about." She told the woman that she wasn't going to give her that information. "Then I'm afraid that I can't help you. Have a good day."

The woman actually hung up on her. Like she had that right. Calling her right back, she repeated what she wanted, careful not to lose her temper right now. When again she asked for her date of birth, Belinda gave it to her but in a whispered voice.

"I can't hear you. Can you repeat that, please? And speak up?" Three more times, she had to repeat her birthdate, and by then, she was screaming it into the phone. "Oh, that will help. Thank you. Mrs. Terrell, is that right?"

"Yes. I want to talk to someone about the mess that is going on in my home. The Federal officers are here, and they've made a huge mess." The woman, she'd not caught her name for the same reason that she'd not the Fed man in the kitchen asked her what they were looking for. "I asked. They said that they were looking around. Also, I want to sue my daughter for custody of my child. Well, she's her child, but I want her as mine so people will stop referring to her as my granddaughter. It's bad enough that people realize that I have a child old enough to call me mother. I don't need the extra baggage of a grandchild right now."

"Mrs. Terrell, were you aware that we were your husband's attorney?" Belinda asked what that had to do with things now. "He was the only one that we worked for. We still do, as a matter of fact. Taking care of his legacy to his children. That would include your granddaughter. This firm has worked for Elliot since his father was working with us on things. I'm sorry to inform you, but you'll have to find other representation on whatever charges that the Federal Government brings to you."

"No. I don't have time for that. You're going to help me out on this. You do know that my husband is dead, don't you? As is his father. I demand that you—" The woman said something, and she had to stop talking to ask her to repeat herself. Belinda was on a roll then and hated that she'd been stopped but what she said to her seemed important enough for her to break her own rule. "What did you say to me about Elliot Terrell? He's dead. I went to his funeral."

"I'm not sure who's funeral you went to, Mrs. Terrell, but Mr. Terrell was just in this office this morning. Apparently, his granddaughter contacted him and told him what was going on, and he decided to open his accounts to help her out. He also left specific instructions that if you were to call and try to retain us on any matter, that he would leave our firm. Mr. Terrell is a good client, and we're, as I said, going to have to turn down helping you out. Again, you have a nice day."

When she hung up this time, Belinda didn't bother calling back. Sitting down on the sofa, she thought about having Elliot, her husband's father around. Christ, he was supposed to be dead. Thinking of the day of his funeral, she wondered what else her husband had lied to her about. Plenty, she was beginning to think.

George had been a good provider, she supposed. She'd never gone without anything that she wanted. There were times that he'd tell her that she was spending too much, but she never paid any attention to him about it. They had money, and she was going to spend it.

After Kerri had been born, he did lavish her with all kinds of gifts. Jewelry, as well as other nice things. She did think about having another child, but it occurred to her that it was going to be hard enough hiding her age when Kerri got older, and she didn't need another child, making her look like one of those women that had fifty children. And there was no way that she was going to look her age at this point in her life. She'd spent too much money and pain on tucks and repairs for her to be called grandma. No. She was going to be beautiful right up until she died.

After her daughter had gotten knocked up with that child, it was impossible for her to be around the two of them without people knowing that she wasn't as young as she wanted people to believe. No amount of surgery to her body would hide a child that called her grandma just to piss her off. Belinda had avoided them as much as she could until Allyson started calling her grannie when they were in public. Smacking her around didn't stop her, either. The child would only get louder when she called out for her. George simply adored them both.

Farley was a nice enough young man, she supposed. But he wasn't good enough for him to be around her and her family. It had taken her nearly eight years to get rid of the man, but she'd been caught killing him by none other than her husband. Killing George hadn't been as easy as it had been to kill the kid. Even though it had been several months ago, about the time that she had her daughter turned out, she remembered it like it was just yesterday.

"What have you done? You've killed that young man." She said that he should be thanking her. "For murdering someone? Christ, Belinda, you've gone too far this time. That young man was helping Kerri raise their daughter. How could you do that to him?"

"Oh, it's not like she loved him. Kerri is incapable of loving anyone but herself." George told her that she had his daughter mixed up with herself. "Perhaps, but he's dead now, and you're going to be the one that will be blamed for it."

He shifted into his large cat and attacked her. If not for the gun that she'd used on the younger man, she might well have been dead too. By shooting George in the head, she was knocked back and hurt badly by falling on a large stick that had been sticking out of the ground.

It had taken her three days to get home, limping all the way before she was able to shift herself and heal. She would have been naked had she done that at the time, and Belinda was sure that would have been more difficult to explain than her being hurt. Had her mate touched her as his cat clawed at her flesh even a little, she'd still be bleeding from the wound and more than likely dead too. Christ, her life has been a fucking nightmare since the day that Allyson had been born.

Now Elliot was still alive. She supposed she should have figured that he was alive. Her husband had told her that there needed to be a closed casket as he'd been in a fiery crash that had taken his father from him. Belinda had wanted to see the old man in death. Simply to make sure that he was actually dead. But since George was so heartbroken over his supposed death, she didn't push the matter. Turns out she should have pushed.

Elliot had hated her from day one. Even at the wedding his parents had paid for, he told her that she'd never get any of his son's money. Nor his. She told him that she'd see about that, and damned if he wasn't correct on that as well. At least his money. She'd yet to find out when the will was going to be read for her husband. That was something else that she needed to check into.

There hadn't been a reading of her mate's will as they had to wait for Kerri to return from her business trip. That was when she hatched the idea that she needed to get rid of the kid as well as her daughter. She hated the fact that people knew when she was with them that she was a grandma. Hatred like she'd never felt before boiled over, and Belinda had taken charge.

"Fat lot of good it had done me." Not only did she not have the kid, but the king of their kind was involved now. "Not that I've done anything that should have him involved in anything I'm working on. It's not like I've broadcast to the world what I've done. Damn it. I hate men."

Well, she did kill her mate and another man. But that wasn't any of anyone's concern but her own. She'd taken care of an issue that she had, and he should be praising her rather than telling her to shut up. That burned her ass when someone had the nerve to talk to her like King Foster had. But there was squat that she could do about it. With him being her king, she was obligated to do what he ordered her to do.

When the Fed joined her in her living room, he sat on her couch like she'd invited him to do it. He simply smiled at her when she told him that he wasn't welcome in her home enough to take liberties with her furniture.

"It's not yours. Nothing in the house, including this couch, is yours. I was just informed that this house isn't in your name. It never has been. When your husband died, the title of it reverted back to his dad, Elliot Terrell. While it was believed that he was dead, we've also been informed that he's not, and he wants you out of his home. This home. As far as that, Mr. Elliot Terrell has asked us to remove you from the premises right now with nothing more than whatever you have on your person as he's been paying for you out of the estate of his sons since—I believe he might be right on this—since you killed your husband. You surely did shit in his oatmeal, didn't you?" He stood up, and Belinda told him that she wasn't going anywhere. That it was her home until she said differently. "As I've explained to you, it's not. You can either leave here on your own two feet, or I take you out the hard way. Knowing you, you're going to make me take you out of here the hard way, aren't you, Belinda?"

"You'll call me Mrs. Terrell, or I'll have your job." He only chuckled at her. "I'm calling my attorney."

"You don't have one." The woman that came

into the room with them looked like she was eating a sandwich that had been in her refrigerator last night. One that she deemed unfit for herself. "I made this one fresh. Yes, I can read your mind. The staff here said that I could have whatever I wanted since you were going to be ousted. I'm Parker Foster. Grand witch. I'd like nothing better than to have you tossed out on your ass, but I promised Kerri, who is nothing like you, thank goodness that I'd play nicely with you. So I'm going to just take you out."

Belinda found herself on the sidewalk in front of her home. Parker suddenly appeared before her, blocking her from going back into the home. As she tried to dance around the other woman, she had a feeling that she was going to be locked out even if she could have gotten by her.

"That's the first truthful thing you've said all day. Yes, you will not be able to get into the house again. If you try, even to touch the doorknob, you'll get a nasty bit of magic that will start to deplete what little magic that you have." She asked her what right did she have to do this to her. "I have every right. Elliot, a man that hates you as much as your daughter seems to said that I was to take out the whore who besmirched his good name and to keep her away from his grandchildren."

"I do hope he understands that they're my family too. As much as I hate to admit it. But I'm not going to take this from any of you. You tell him that he's not to get too comfortable as I'm going to make sure he's dead this time." She asked if she'd just threatened him. "Are you going to tell on me, Parker? I don't care. I know my own rights, and I'm going to see to it that you're punished too. Whoever is above you, they'll be hearing from me."

"I'm in charge of everything that has to do with witchcraft, dumbass. Perhaps you don't understand what 'grand witch' means. I'm the most powerful one in the world." Belinda snorted at her. "Very mature. I would think that a woman nearing seventy would have better manners than that."

"I'm nowhere near seventy, you bitch." She felt a pinch to her face and reached up when it felt like it was sagging. "What the hell did you do to me? Do you know how much money it cost for me to have my face redone? You're going to put it back right now, or so help me, I'm going to sue you."

"You have fun with that." The woman

disappeared. Just as she was going to stomp right up to her home and demand that they let her in, she felt the woman in her mind. *"You're going to lose one thing that you had done to your body each time you go near Allyson and the rest of my family. That would include all the Fosters as well as anyone else we deemed family. I'm thinking that it'll take a while before you're actually showing your age, as you've had a lot of body repair done to yourself. Do they give you numbers to come by and pick up the pieces that they had to take off? Kind of like they do in a car shop? Something to think about."*

Belinda was about as pissed as she'd ever been in her life. The house was off limits to her for now, so there was no way for her to see what sort of damage had been done to her face. Christ, she must look a sight. It was then that she noticed when touching her skin that only one side of her face was sagging again. It was just too much. She was going to be killing off a lot of people before this was done, and she was going to start with that fucking grand bitch.

~*~

The house was beautiful. There wasn't much in the way of furniture, but she didn't mind that. She was happy, too, that Allyson was able to pick out her own room so quickly. The fact that there were bunk beds in the room, along with a large desk, is what sealed the deal for her. Kerri loved the kitchen too.

"I've had Rogue hire us a staff. We're going to need them in the coming months, so she's going to do background checks on them before they come to work for us." She nodded, wondering how much money Keegan had. "Also, your accounts have been opened up. Not just the bank but all of them. That was Brooks doing. She said that there wasn't any reason for them to have been sealed in the first place."

"I have money. A great deal of it. I'm not sure how much you have, but we'll combine them, right?" Keegan told her that whatever he had was hers and that what she had was hers as well. "That's not the way that it works for me. We share everything. All right?"

"Yes, of course." She had a feeling that he was humoring her but let it go. "I know that you've contacted your grandfather. He's been making waves for your mother. The house that she shared with your dad is being gone through by the Feds. She's been kicked out because the house is in your grandfather's name since your father passed away. They're doing a clean sweep of it to find evidence, then it's going to be stripped down to the walls and redecorated by a firm. He wants every part of Belinda out of his life."

"What happened to Boytoy?" Keegan laughed and told her that he had left the state. "Good for him. Even though my mother implicated him in taking my child, Allyson said that all he did was stand there looking like a dork. I think that he was caught up in something that he had no control over with my mother."

"That's what Parker told me." She nodded and moved around the living room they'd ended up in. "What's the matter? You seemed to be lost or something. Is there anything that I can do to help you?"

"I don't know what's wrong. Well, that's not true. I'm overwhelmed. I know that you guys are, too, but all this shit that my mother has done is really taking its toll on me. And I'm only just realizing that while I know that she's my mother, I don't think that I've ever liked her. Isn't that sad?" Keegan said that it wasn't and told her about his own father. "We have a lot more in common than I thought. Mostly I'm worried about my daughter. Our daughter. She's putting on a brave face right now, but I'm worried that it's going to hit her soon that all this is because my mother didn't want her."

"I love you, mom." Allyson came to her then. Hugging her tightly to her, Keegan left them there. "Belinda, because I'm not going to call her grandma ever again, is a bad person. I don't love her. I don't like her either. The things that she did to take us apart will never be anything that I can get over. You should just let it go and let the Fosters take charge."

"She's going to be in big trouble with not just the police but with the pride as well." Allyson told her that she liked Uncle Ronan. "So you've adopted them, have you? From what I'm to understand, they've adopted you too. I don't understand why they'd want to do that. You're nothing but a pain in my butt all the time."

They were still laughing when Keegan came into the room with her grandda. Getting up, she hugged him to her and told him how much she missed him. Then she introduced her grandda to her daughter. He hugged Allyson too.

"When your pop was alive, he'd send me pictures all the time. We couldn't tell anyone, of course, but I've been keeping up with your lives all along. When he was murdered, I've no doubt that the bitch killed him. It nearly took me along with him. My goodness, you sure are the spitting image of your grandma, my mate, honey." The two of them hugged, and grandda sat down on the couch with her. Keegan left them again, telling them that he had to talk to his brother. "He's a good man, that one. Told me right off the bat that he was going to make sure that you were forever happy. I believe him."

"You'll stay here with us, won't you, grandda? I've missed you so much." He told her that he'd been told that he was staying. At least until this thing with Belinda was taken care of. "Forever. I want you to stay with us forever. You've a lot of catching up to do with your great-granddaughter. And who knows, you might be having more little ones around soon too."

Looking at Keegan when he returned, he winked at her. She realized that she'd already fallen in love with him. Getting up to sit next to him, Kerri leaned her head on his shoulder. There was a connection between the two of them that she was only just noticing. Not just between the two of them as humans, but their lions seemed to be as well.

"How about we have some dinner delivered? Where I was staying, I couldn't have anything delivered, and I have to tell you, I've missed that." Keegan asked her grandda what he was craving. "Just about anything that I can sink my teeth into. Meat, of course. Chinese is my favorite. Pizza too."

Keegan laughed. "It just so happens that we have all those kinds of places right here in town. I'll take care that we have plenty to eat." When he left them again, he was pulling out his cell phone. She looked over at her daughter and grandda.

"I'm in love with him." Grandda laughed, and Allyson rolled her eyes at her. "Well, it's been forever since anyone has been there for me, and it's taken me a bit to get my crap together."

"Mom, I love you to pieces, but you're never going to have your crap together until you learn to tell people you need help." She stood up then and looked at her great-grandda. "How about you and I figure out where you're going to be staying while you're here. Close to my room, I'm hoping. Keegan has an amazing library here too."

Left alone in the living room, she leaned back on

the couch. Her heart hurt. Not for what her daughter had said to her but that her mother had done this to them. The more she thought about the chain of events, she realized that without her mother being a royal bitch, then she might well not have met Keegan and his family. Her grandda would still be hidden away. Her daughter? Well, she couldn't think along those lines about what might have happened to her little girl. She knew that she was safe. More than likely for the first time in her young life. As was she.

Kerri woke up to someone saying her name. Keegan stood over her, and he had the most beautiful smile. Pulling him to her, she kissed him. It wasn't sexual in any way, but it was comforting. Just what she needed.

"As much as I'd like to pursue this more, the food is here. We'd better hurry before the other two eat it all before we get there." She stood up with him. Feeling slightly dizzy, she held onto him until she was able to stand steady. "Careful there. You don't want to hurt yourself. Come on and eat. It's been a while, and I'm betting that you're a little weak from not having much to eat today."

There was more than enough for her to fill up on,

she noticed. There were four large pizzas that looked to have double the meat on them. About twenty large and small white boxes with oriental writing on them. There were subs from her favorite shop, soda and water bottles, as well as a huge tray of fruit. She noticed that Keegan had some of everything on his plate. Sitting down, she was glad to see that Allyson also had a nice sampling of the food as well as fruit. Her grandda had a beer. Something that she knew that he enjoyed when he was having pizza.

They feasted. There was no other word for how they polished off not just all the little boxes of Chinese food but also the better part of all four pizzas. They decided, even though she didn't think she'd have any room left, that they'd go into town for ice cream. Also, to see the lights.

The town had gone all out for the holidays. She'd noticed it, of course, when she'd been trying to secure a place to stay where it was warm and food to eat. However, this was so much better. Each of the shops were decorated in bright lights and colors. The snow was the perfect touch to the shops, and she and Allyson entered the one that had a huge display out front about having new ornaments in.

She'd never enjoyed Christmas before. No, she told herself. It wasn't that she didn't enjoy it. It was that she never allowed herself to enjoy it. Working too hard and too many hours kept her away from her home life as well as her daughter. Kerri couldn't even remember the last time that she and Allyson had sat down to a meal together. It had been made impossible by working so much. She wasn't going to allow herself to do that again. And now she had Keegan to make memories with, and she was going to do everything to make it so they were the best she could make.

They ended up getting four ornaments each. Allyson had picked out a couple of items that she wanted to get for her new family, and it was easy enough for her to have them sent to the home she now shared with Keegan. Everyone in town seemed to know that she and Keegan were mates, and they were so nice to her.

This was going to be a new beginning for her and Allyson. They were going to spend more time together and enjoy life. It had been one of the things that had kept her living when her mother had turned her out of everything that she'd had. She promised herself that she was going to live every single day like it was her last. It had felt that way a few times, but now she was here and going strong. Thanks fully to Keegan and his family.

Chapter 3

Keegan put the last file in the drawer and closed it. It had taken him nearly four hours to get them in the right cabinets and longer than that to figure out that he was going to need to hire someone to answer his phone and generally help him out with filing files as well. He thought about just putting a recording on his phone, telling people that he was working for a private company and wasn't taking on new clients. However, he thought that to be rude, and one thing that Keegan wasn't, was rude to strangers.

When it rang again, he just let it go. Keegan figured that he was wasting about ten minutes each time he had to go and answer it, so he simply didn't.

As soon as the person on the other end hung up, he picked up the phone and turned the ringer off. It was too much to let him concentrate on his job.

"How's it going?" He smiled at Brook when she spoke from behind him. "I'm assuming that it's going well. I have a couple of things that I'd like for you to go over for me. This is the most important thing I have bothering me. The numbers aren't adding up on this, and I've been looking at it too long for me to be able to figure it out on my own." She handed him the file then he handed it back to her.

"You don't pay forty million dollars for grass seed, do you?" She looked at the paperwork and cursed. "Like you said, someone else looking at something helps. I've been thinking about how to separate the businesses from the personal accounts that I'm going over for all of us. I don't know that there is much in the way of personal to even bother with, do you?"

"Doubtful. I mean, other than a few bills to do with the houses, I don't think any of us have any projects on our own. Even the Party House is in the family books even though your mother owned the building and the land that it's on." He said that his mom wanted him to keep track of it so that they don't run over budget. "She's very worried about that. I told her that we had plenty enough money to take care of the building. I believe that's what made her come on board with charging even a little bit of money to use the building. She has decided that she's going to come up with a family plan to use the pool that won't hurt even the poorest of homes."

"I spoke to her about that. After telling her what insurance would be on both the pool and the House, she decided that was a great deal of money not to have help on. I suggested that she have a sliding scale on the amount to charge people per their income and family size. She said that she was going to talk it over with the family when we get together tonight. Is dinner still on at your home?" She told him that it was. They were having comfort food. "That's my favorite next to steaks on the grill. What is this comfort food that we're having so I know to save room for it?"

"Beef and homemade noodles. Mashed potatoes, lima beans with sour cream and dill and some other sides. For dessert, we're having a sampling of things that I'd like to have out for

Christmas. Since the Thanksgiving dinner went over
so well, we're going to do that again for the town
for Christmas. Your mom said that it might be the
only time that some of the families here in town get a
hot meal. I want to do something about that as well."
Keegan laughed and begged her not to start another
project this year. "Ronan told me the same thing. We
have too many projects going on now. I have hired
twenty-five more people to work the greenhouse
for me. It's growing faster than I thought it would.
We'll have seedlings starting in March and trees for
late April. The land I purchased just after Allen and
Cindy were put back in prison for the rest of their
lives is working out better than I thought it would."

Keegan sometimes forgot about Brook's family.
They'd been horrific people, trying to kill Brook
off so that they could get the insurance that they'd
taken out on her and inherit the house that they'd
been living in. This was after they'd killed both her
parents. All the families he was beginning to realize
hadn't come from good backgrounds. But they sure
made up for it when they met their family and made
them stronger.

Keegan went over a few things with her

that he'd been looking into. There wasn't just the books that he was keeping for her and all the other businesses, but he'd also been making sure that funding for their charities was being taken care of as well. Not just that there was plenty of money to fund them, but that the money was being used for what it had been set up for as well. They had more than enough charities to keep him busy on a daily basis.

"You're going to need help in here, Keegan. While I know you're keeping on top of things for us, I don't want you to be working all the time. Not with you having a new mate and child in the house." He told her that he'd been thinking the same thing just before she came in. "I did notice that you turned the phone off. I'm not even sure why you wanted one in." He told her. "Oh. I guess I never thought of that. Having access when something happens at one of the projects would be a good thing for you to know about. And since I rarely go over budget when we're working, I can see where it would come in handy, too, so that you can shut work off when you leave here. Good job on that. I'll see about getting you set up on the service that we have at the house too. That way, when you just want to take a day off, you can without being bothered unless it's an emergency."

"Thank you." She wandered around the office, and he let her. After all, this was her building anyway. When she paused at the window that looked out over the street, she started talking.

"Belinda has killed before George and Farley. Not a great many deaths, mind you but enough that she needs to be taken care of before anyone else dies. I know that's what we thought she'd done when she so easily killed them off, but it's far worse than I think any of us could have imagined." When she didn't say anything more, he waited. Keegan wasn't sure if he really wanted to know or not. But he also knew that he would need to know for Kerri and Allyson. "She's been selling off children that are at an orphanage not far from here. So far, I've been able to track fifteen children, all under the age of ten, that have mysteriously disappeared from the care given at the home. While that doesn't sound like a great number, that's only the ones that I could track as being in the home and disappearing." She turned to him. "I've found out that Allyson was on that list that was to be shipped out to be turned over to a group of pedophiles that she *helps* out with children."

"Christ." He sat down and then stood up. "Does Kerri know this? I mean, anyone other than you and Ronan knows about this?"

"No. I wanted to let you know first so you could be there for Kerri when she's told. I don't want Allyson to know. Though I have to admit, I think she might know a little more than we think. She was at the house long enough for her to have heard a great deal about her grandmother's dealings." Keegan nodded, thinking about how this was going to hurt his little family. "I can't attach Belinda to any of the missing children as having any part of them being gone. She owns the building, yes, but other than that, she could say that she rented it out for the use that it says on the front door but she didn't know what was going on. But Parker looked into her mind and found it for me. It's right there in her mind how she's going to have to get there and get her some money. And give them the list of children that she wants to go out in the next shipment. I'm afraid that she's going to be looking for little ones to go out so that she can have some ready cash to run with. That scares me more than anything, and I find myself keeping a closer eye on children when I'm out. Christ, that woman is a fucking bitch."

"Have you found the children, Brook? You said fifteen children. Do you know where they are?" She nodded, then she shook her head. "They're dead, aren't they? She sold them off, and then they were killed. Christ, that is sadder than anything that I've ever seen before. I'm surprised that she didn't put her own daughter into that ring."

"I don't think it was for lack of trying. I'm thinking that had her husband not been there all the time, she might well have. You've heard how Belinda goes on about being a grandma. I'm thinking that she would have had the same issues with being a mother of a grown daughter too." He thought about Kerri telling him that her mother had dressed her in younger children's clothing as she got older and knew that would have been her plan to rid herself of Kerri. Keegan asked Brook if there was more. "Yes. Most of it is petty when compared to the selling of the children, but I think when we have George exhumed in the next few days, it'll bring to light how she was the one that killed him. Parker said that the bullet from either man wasn't removed for some reason. I have an idea that it was something that Belinda had a weighted hand in."

"I do as well. Are you going to exhume Farley too?" She told him how they were still trying to get in touch with his parents to ask. "I think that Allyson should be able to do that for you. She's a minor, but so long as Kerri gives her the okay to ask for it, then she can have it done. It might be stretching the law a little, but I'm thinking that it can be done. Especially if you find a judge that is willing to bend the rules for you a little."

She kissed him on the cheek. While he was happy to help her, he did ask her what that was for. Instead of answering him, she kissed him again. Keegan was still laughing when she left him there to take care of a few things for this to happen. Going to his office, he worked on the few things that he still had to finish up. It was Allyson who interrupted him this time. They'd been in town shopping for Christmas decorations, and he wasn't surprised to see her coming into his office.

"Mom wants to know what you know about the pack school that is near where Uncle Ronan lives. She thinks that I'll be safer there than in a public school. I'm all for homeschooling again, but I think

Mom thinks I need a social group to hang out with."
She rolled her eyes. "I don't think she's noticed that
there are about four thousand people in your family
that I hang out with just fine."

"I think she's thinking that you need to hang
out with kids your own age." She told him that kids
her age thought she was a nerd. "Yes, I know that
feeling. My childhood was much like that too. But
they called me a number worm. I never understood
that one, but that's what you get for liking to deal
with numbers. I tell you what, I'm nearly finished
here. We can go over there if you want. We can see
what sort of classes they have to offer."

She was all for that. And when Kerri joined
them, they decided that they'd walk. All of them
being cats, it was nice to share the cold outside with
someone of the like body temperature. They even got
to play in the snow a little bit while walking there.

He loved the pack that was on their lands.
Most of the time, they'd help them with projects that
required someone to watch over something for a bit.
The wolves were a loyal group, and since a great
many of them were friends with Brook, they were
willing to help with anything as she was forever

providing them with jobs as well as funding when they needed it.

"Harvard, I'd like for you to meet my mate and daughter, Kerri and Allyson. Ladies, this is Harvard Luna. Pack master to one of the oldest packs in the United States." He shook both their hands and smiled. "Allyson is in need of a place to learn that will keep her safe from outside forces. Her grandmother, as a matter of fact."

"I've heard about her. Not as much as I'm sure you have, but she's been sniffing around here for a couple of days. We've had a good time running her off. She never shifts and comes back on the wolves that I send after her. Do you suppose she has trouble with that?" Keegan hadn't thought about that but was going to check into it when he was with Ronan again. "Allyson, what is it you're interested in? We have a plethora of classes here that aren't what you'd learn in a regular school setting. There are other classes, such as literature and math, but we also have a great many classes that have to do with survival in the woods, as well as old-school things such as weaving baskets. Dying wool. Things that come in handy more than you think."

Keegan could see her excitement when he mentioned the other classes that they would offer her. As soon as one of Harvard's sons joined them, Allyson went with Joey to sit in some of the classes with him. Harvard asked them if they had a few minutes to spare.

"Yes. Always for you." He sat down with them at the large table inside his pack house. "I'm assuming that's why Joey took Allyson away. Whatever you have to tell us is about Belinda sniffing around."

"It is. She's been trying to take some of the younger ones from here. We've caught her three times on the land, but it wasn't until this last time that we figured out what she was here for. Once one of the younger wolves took a bit of her blood, it was easy enough to figure out that she wanted the pups to sell off. That was a real eye-opener for me and the other members." Keegan looked at Kerri when Harvard spoke. "You knew about this then."

"Not until about an hour ago." Kerri asked him if he'd been planning on telling her about it. "I was. However, if you remember, you told me just this morning that you didn't want to be told a single thing about Belinda today. That it was for Allyson."

"I did. But this is something that I should have been told." Harvard said he was sorry. "No, don't be. I guess I shouldn't be surprised by what she was going to do. I think it was her plan for me when I was younger. I never actually wanted to believe that she was going to do it, but—holy Christ, she was going to sell off Allyson too. Wasn't she?"

"Parker found it in her head when she was seeing what she'd been up to. However, without proof, actual proof, there isn't any way that we can have her arrested. I'm not sure that Ronan can't do something about it, but we were going to talk to you tonight at the house. I'm sorry I didn't tell you, but I really did want you to have a good day with Allyson. I think you both needed it." She agreed with him. Keegan looked at Harvard again. "What do you know about the kids being nearly taken? What was the way that she did it? I mean, like, did she hurt them first? I would need details so that I can tell Ronan. We can work together on this and get her out of our hair."

"Can Ronan make her confess to the police?" Keegan told Kerri that he could but again, without some sort of proof, there wasn't much the police could go on. "I suppose. I hate that she's getting away with this."

"She's not." Harvard laughed before continuing. "I have three of my best men on her all the time now. She's being watched night and day to keep her out of things like buildings that don't belong to her. They've managed to chase her out of a couple of them that you guys own. As well as shoplifting. I think she's getting hungry and stupider."

"She isn't really stupid, is she? I mean, she's not been caught at doing what she's been doing for however long she's been taking kids, right? But we do need to get her off the streets. And soon before she hurts someone else." Taking Kerri's hand into his, he was glad that she was taking this so well. "I'm going to have to talk to Allyson about this too. She needs to know that she has to be extra careful from now on."

"Yes. She'll be safe here. I'll have people around her at all times." They talked about the things going on between the two groups. Keegan was glad that he'd brought up him needing help around his office. Harvard said that he had four women, all of them secretaries from the city, that had come home for one reason or another. "You said there are four of them.

I'm not sure that I'd have that much work for them to all work for me."

"They're breeding. I'm so happy to say that. It's been a while since—never mind. I was thinking that you could hire the four of them as part-timers and let them work around the schedule that you'd need them for. That's what another group did working on construction. Not breeding, but they were working in the school too, and it worked out well for everyone. I think that Brook might well have come up with that idea." Keegan said he'd have to talk to her about it. "She's a good woman too. All the Foster women are. I'm glad to have gotten to meet you, Kerri. And if you'd allow it, we'll make sure that your little girl is safe as if you were watching over her."

"I'm glad to know that. However, it'll be up to her if she wants to come here. I do worry about her a great deal. Especially in light of what I've just found out about Belinda." Harvard told her that he was sorry about that. "Don't be. Please. I needed to know, no matter how I found out about it. Thank you for that."

When Allyson joined them with Joey, Keegan could tell that she loved the classes. She went on about them all the way back to their house. How she was going to be able to take some classes that would benefit her above all other classes that she'd get in a school building. However, as soon as they were home, he had a feeling that something had happened. Elliot met them in the front hall as soon as they had their coats off.

"Your mother is dead, Kerri. I'm so sorry."

~*~

Kerri rocked in the chair that was in the bedroom that she'd been sleeping in. Knowing that her mother was dead didn't help her nerves right now. What bothered her the most was how she'd been killed. It wasn't quick nor without a great deal of bloodshed. Shaking her head, she wasn't bothered by it so much but that it had come to the point where she had to be put down like she had been.

Grandda had told her everything that he knew. That Belinda had tried to take Jasper and Bethy's children right out of their stroller. Twin little boys that had more magic surrounding them than her mother had sense in her head. Just as she got a foot from them, Jasper, in all his glory, went after her and killed her. Over and over again until Bethy stopped him.

"I'm sorry, my lady." She looked at the big fae and smiled at him. He'd been in the living room when she'd come up here to talk to Allyson. If someone were to ask her, she'd not be able to tell them how she'd ended up in the bedroom at all. But now that Jasper was here, she knew that of all the people she needed to speak to, it was him. "She meant to take my sons."

"I'm glad that you saved them, Jasper. You've no idea how sorry I am that she even tried. And if you're saying you're sorry, again, that you killed her, then I am going to have to smack you around. Being magical or not, I will harm you. You did what you had to do to protect your children. I would have done no less had she tried to take my child again." He sat down on the footstool that was in front of her. "I'm sure that this sounds terrible, coming from her daughter, but I'm so relieved that she's gone that I can't even express myself. She was a horrible person, and the world is better off without her being around."

"Thank you. So much." He looked around the room and then back at her. "My mother is grateful for your forgiveness in this as well. And that you have no hard feelings toward me. She's fallen in love with our boys, and I believe it would have broken her had she lost me as well. You know that you could have ordered my death, and it would have been well within your rights to do so."

"I don't want to talk about that part, Jasper. I'm glad. Not just that you're safe, but your children and mate are as well. I like Bethy. And you and your sons. I want you to just go on like I wasn't related to that person at all, and we'll be just fine." He nodded but looked around again. "Is there something that I'm missing here? You seem to be very preoccupied with this room."

"My mother is grateful for your forgiveness, as I said. She has a gift for you." She told him that she didn't need a gift. He'd done all the hard work. "Nay, you have given me a great gift in not blaming me. She wishes to talk to you and to give you something." He smiled. "You must understand that to not accept a gift from a queen is frowned upon."

"Oh well then—hold on. Did you say, queen? Your mother is the queen of…Jasper. Is your mother the queen of the fae?" He nodded and stood up. When he bowed, she stood to do the same.

"Oh, do get up, the two of you. I know just how Ronan feels when someone does that to him. Get up off the floor, Kerri and give me a hug." She did so, but not without a bit of laughter. She was in the presence of a great queen and didn't know just how to act. "You're to act like we're old friends and leave it at that. My goodness, you are a beauty, aren't you? Your daughter must be just as lovely. Now, I have a gift for you."

"Straight to the point. I like that in a person. However, just as I was telling your son, I don't need a gift from you. I would enjoy your friendship, but a gift isn't necessary." She told her that it was to her. "Then I'd say we should get this over with so that—hang on? This isn't going to be something I can hang in my room to remember you by, is it?"

"No, child, it will not." The touch to her heart nearly had her asking if that was it. Her touch was warm, her finger strong as it touched her. When something powerful rolled over her, she felt her bones shake, and her teeth rattle in her head. "You're going to be all right, Kerri. Just fine indeed."

That was the last thing she heard as her head exploded in pain. Then she slipped into unconsciousness, and that was it for her. She knew that she was dying and that it was all her fault for agreeing to take a gift from the queen.

"I don't give a good fuck why she's out. I want her to wake the fuck up and tell me she's all right." Kerri didn't move when she heard Keegan talking to someone. Yelling more like it, but she didn't move. "You said that you gave her a gift of magic. You didn't tell her that it was going to change her."

"Kerri, please tell your mate that you are well." She looked at the two people in the room with her. "There. See? She's just fine. As I told you several times." Keegan growled, and Kerri laughed.

"What the hell happened to me?" She sat up and laid back down when dizziness swamped her. "I think that you broke me."

"Nay, I did nothing of the sort. I have enhanced you. As I was telling Keegan here before he got it in his head to yell at me, you have a bit of magic already before I gave you more. It was long ago. Longer than there have been shifters of lions in this realm." Keegan asked her how that was possible. "It is possible as she is right here before you. Why must you question my every word, young man? Do you not respect that I'm much older than even the oldest of the shifters?"

"I question you about this because you did something to my mate that scared the shit out of me." She put her hand on his heart, and Kerri could see the calmness roll over him. "Thank you for that. But that doesn't negate the fact that you should have told us what you were going to be doing to her. All right?"

"I didn't know that she was already magical. Other than the fact that she's gotten magic from you as a couple. Also, I have to tell you that the two of you would be so much more powerful if you were to bond. Sooner rather than later. As I have said to you several times now." The queen was getting frustrated, and Kerri thought it was funny. When she turned to look at her, the smile on her face wasn't all that friendly. "You're going to have to call me by my first name eventually, you know. It's Andonna. And your relative from long ago, he was fae. You've gotten all his magic that has been sleeping within you since you were a babe. If I had had time, without your mate badgering me, I might well have been able to figure out some things. If you would be so kind, my child, you need to drink more juice while I search."

She disappeared, and Kerri looked at Keegan. He looked about as pissed off as she was confused. Laughing at him, she asked him to join her on the bed, and he didn't hesitate but stripped down and got into the bed with her.

"Much better." She wrapped herself around him and held him tightly to her. "You have entirely too many clothes on. Let me take care of that for you, my dear mate."

Chapter 4

Keegan took his time in taking off her clothing. Unbuttoning each button gave him a piece of her that he'd not as yet touched. Kissed or tasted. When she was nearly naked beneath him, he leaned over to her belly and kissed her there.

She moaned when he nipped at her navel and then swirled his tongue in the indentation. She put her hand on his head and curled her fingers into his thick hair making Keegan moan with pleasure. The silkiness of her flesh made him run his fingers from the front to the back before she gripped him again.

"I need to taste you, Kerri. I want to see if you taste as wonderful as you smell." He jerked her panties off her, and she cried out again when he nipped at her thigh.

Her body was responding before he could even tell her how much he wanted from her. Keegan was between her legs, which he'd put on either side of his head before she could protest if she was ever going to. As soon as he pulled her clit into his mouth, she cried out his name and came. Never had anything made him feel this way. No amount of sex could have prepared him for making love to his mate. Christ, Keegan thought, he was in love with his beautiful mate.

He ate her like he was never going to stop. The more he took from her, the more he gave her, the more she seemed to want. Every time he bit down on her, she came crying out his name. Every time he slid his tongue into her sheath, Kerri was soaking him with her juices. When he slid his fingers into her, she rode his hand, her hips coming up off the bed like he was fucking her.

"Come for me again. Come and let me drink from you again." She laid back, her body so taunt with need that when he sucked her clit into his mouth as he stretched her with his fingers, she bowed up off the bed and screamed. He never stopped taking her, even when she begged him to stop with one breath, then begged him for more with the next.

When he stood up over her, he could see her need. It was like a mask over her face, showing him how much she wanted him. And the thought of him taking her was nearly his undoing. He knew that it was going to hurt her with him wanting her so desperately. So, instead of sliding into her like they both wanted, he fisted his cock until long streams of his precum fell onto her.

Keegan moaned when she reached for him. "Honey, you touch me, and it's going to be over right now. I want to come all over you. Have my cum spray all over your pretty pussy until you come again. Tell me you want it. Tell me, Kerri, tell me you want me."

"Please." He leaned over her and took her mouth. He could feel the head of his cock just at her entrance, where it was wet and warm. When he bowed back, lifting his head from her, he roared out as he filled her, his cock slamming into her until she screamed with her own release. Over and over, he took her hard until there was simply nothing left of him. But still, he gave her as much pleasure as he could. Holding her body as he filled her.

Kerri came several times in those moments as well. Each time she cried out, he could only hold her tightly in his arms. When his body seemed to be revving up for another release, he held onto Kerri with both hands as he emptied deeply within her until he could only drop on her from exhaustion.

As she came with him this time, he felt a wave of darkness roll over him. Like he'd been painted in her release, and the two of them were one. When she whimpered again, he looked down at her and smiled.

"That was fantastic." He thanked her. "Yes, because it was all about you. Dork. Christ, Keegan, I don't know if I'll be able to move again. Why on earth were we not doing this every night?"

"Life. Mostly that. But there is the little matter of finding you alone. We do seem to be going in different directions a lot." She pulled the blankets up and over the two of them. "I do hope that Andonna doesn't return anytime too soon. I need a long—"

Keegan knew that it was magic that made his head feel slightly off. As his body began to hurt, like his skin was being peeled off his body, he tried to pull away from Kerri so that whatever happened, he didn't hurt her. When she cried out in pain, he knew that whatever was coming to them was powerful. Not only that, but he was reasonably sure that it was going to put the two of them out for a few hours, if not for days.

Blood began to slide down his arms to the bed. As much as he wanted to help Kerri, to make sure that she wasn't hurting too much, he couldn't. Keegan knew that on some level that if he were to open his mouth, he would have screamed in pain. His body, not feeling like it was going to make it reached up and slapped him out of consciousness. If he was honest with himself, he was glad to be out.

When he woke up, he was lying in bed with Kerri. She had her eyes open, but he could see that she'd been crying. As he started to reach for her, to see if she was all right, he saw the markings on his wrist that went up and over his shoulder. Touching his finger to Kerri, she looked at him and then turned away just as quickly.

"Look at me, please." She didn't, and he said her name again. "Kerri, honey, please look at me so I can see how badly you're hurting."

"I don't know what happened. One minute I was ready to doze off. The next, I was writhing in pain. Are you all right?" He said that, like her, he was afraid to check. That made her giggle. "I'm thinking that whatever happened, it has a lot to do with Andonna. Do you suppose she found out who my late relative was and zapped us? I don't know any other reason for her to have done that to us. Do you?"

"I don't think that she'd do that. Not without a better reason than a long lost relative. However, she gifted you magic, and whatever you had before— which she said was sleeping within you when we bonded, it woke it up, and you shared it with me." Kerri told him she liked that better. "I do as well. I'd not like to think that a queen of anyone would be vindictive about something you had no control over."

He looked at his arm and was amazed at how tatted it was. Upon looking at it better after setting up, he realized that it wasn't a tat but a sigil. Keegan was surprised, too, to figure out that it was in fae, a language that he'd not been able to read before. Now not only could he understand what was written on him, but he could also remember each of the lines of his life easily. Looking over at Kerri when she sat up as well, he asked her if she could read it.

"Yes. It looks like it's about me. It even has on here the day that Allyson was born and the time." She looked at him. "I think we need to get dressed and have a conversation with Andonna. I don't mind that it's here, though I think I'll have a hard time explaining it at the Parent Teachers conferences, but that's all right, too, I guess. I wonder if Allyson got any of this."

They made their way downstairs after taking a shower together. It might well have been quicker if they'd taken one separately, but he was glad too that he'd been able to take Kerri again against the walls of the stall. Arriving down in the kitchen before she was, he kissed Allyson on the forehead as he walked by her.

"A woman called here about an hour ago. She said that Brook hired her to be our cook. I didn't know anything about it, so I told her that she'd have to call back later in the morning." Keegan glanced at the clock and saw that it was nearly seven already. "I'm going to be picked up at seven-thirty to spend the day at the pack school. Joey, he's a nice kid, by the way, told me that I'd only have to bring paper and pens with me to take notes on things. I'd not be required to do any homework or such until I decide what I want to do. Would it be all right with you if I were to go there? I know mom and you suggested it, but I want to make sure before I get too excited about some of the classes."

"I think that it would be good for you to be there. I'm not sure what sort of things you might have gotten growing up as a lion from your family, but it never hurts to find out about other shifters too." He asked her about the markings on himself. Did she have any similar ones. "Your mom was told yesterday, I guess last night, that she has a little fae in her bloodline. That would include you as well. When we can get in touch with Andonna, the queen of fae, again, we're going to sit down with her and figure out what that means for us as a family. I'm assuming a great deal since we both got a significant amount of magic."

While she finished up her breakfast, Keegan kissed Kerri on the mouth when she joined them in the kitchen. He was making eggs and bacon for the two of them when Ronan and Brook showed up. After about ten minutes of talking about nothing really, Allyson was picked up and taken to the pack house. She was going to be staying there all day, and even though Belinda was dead, they still wanted her to be as safe as possible.

"All right. Tell us what you're trying very hard not to upset us about." Kerri sat down with a glass of juice and looked at him before continuing to speak to Ronan. "Is it bad? If so, I think you should just spill it. I don't want to have to deal with bullshit today."

"All right. Let's get right to the point. Your mother wasn't a born lion. According to the records that go back for centuries on everyone that is a lion, she was born to lions but someplace in her lineage, there was a human in the family. Did you ever see your mom as a lion?" Kerri asked Ronan if he was sure about that. "I am. The book that I got when I became the king of lions is magical. When a lion is born or dies, it's written in the book as to not only their parents but the time of birth and who was present at the death. Also, I didn't know this until I pulled the book out that it also has their magical powers given to them at the time of birth. Your mother was never able to shift as the gene that was human prevented her from being able to do that."

"I guess I never thought about it. I mean, I know that my dad and I would go running when I was younger. But it never occurred to me that she couldn't shift with us. I just assumed, like I always did about my mother, she didn't want to be seen with us and declined to play around." Ronan told her that there was more and Keegan took her hand into his as they waited on Ronan. "Is it about my father's murder?"

"She killed them both. Farley's family has been made aware of his murder, and he's been buried in the family cemetery. I didn't know that he was a lion as well until I looked into his death. I'm sure that you knew that she killed them both, but it's been confirmed. And even though she's dead, her name as a lion has been stricken from the records. It's still in the book about her birth and death, even that Jasper was the one that justly killed her, but she won't be given a place in the book as a good standing member of the lion pride." She asked him what happens now. "It's whatever you want to happen. What I mean is, she was a murderer, not even counting the deaths of the children she had a hand in killing. Since Jasper killed her, there wasn't much of her left to have been buried anyway. However, I will tell you that you're going to inherit her estate, and there was quite a bit of it when she died. I've also had the orphanage closed down, and the building will be destroyed within the next few days. I'm sorry if that isn't anything—"

"No. You're right in doing that. It should have been destroyed years ago." Keegan watched as Kerri paced. He looked at his brother.

"I'd like to see if there is anything that Farley's family needs. I hate that this happened to their son, but I'd like to make sure that they're compensated for what happened to him." Ronan said that they'd already taken care of it out of the funds set up for such a thing. "They're still alive, I take it? Both of them?"

"They never wanted anything to do with Allyson. I don't know why but he told me that they were just happy that he wasn't going to marry me." Kerri laughed, but it was forced and hurtful sounding. "It's their loss. But Farley was in Allyson's life every day. He'd even take her on runs with him when he was out. However, he never took her to his parents as they didn't like the fact that my mom was who she was."

"I can understand that." She nodded at him, and Keegan looked at Ronan. "When you notified them, did you tell them that Belinda was dead? I would imagine that it would be a great relief to them just knowing that justice was served."

"I did. And they'd like to meet Allyson. I told them what I thought you'd say and that it would be up to you and your daughter. I don't know what their plans are with this meeting, I could ask Parker to look and see, but when I told them how Belinda was dead, they seemed unusually relieved." Keegan asked if perhaps Belinda had harmed them in addition to killing their son. "I don't know. As I said, they were unusually happy at her death and right away asked if I'd ask you about Allyson."

"Do you suppose that Belinda threatened them in some way if they were a part of Allyson's life? I didn't know her all that well, but I can see her doing that to someone." Kerri said she'd not put it past her, either. "It's something to think about. I don't know what she could have said to them to put them off, but I'm betting that it was horrific."

"I'll have Parker look into that for you." Kerri asked when she was to contact them about seeing Allyson. "I didn't give them any kind of date that I would talk to you about it. As you can imagine, they're older now, and I'd say that they were in poor health. I'm betting too that a great deal of that has to be because of the death of their only child."

"Let me know what Parker can find out." Kerri then asked Ronan if there was anything else. "You said that there was her estate. If you'd asked me, I'd of thought that she wouldn't have had all that much after grandda tossed her out of the house."

"There were insurance policies that were your father's. They've never been cashed, as they named you as a beneficiary. It's a large amount because his death has been ruled as a murder. Also, Farley left some inheritance to Allyson that I've been made aware of." She asked if she could talk to her daughter about what to do with that. "Yes. I expected no less of you to do that."

After Ronan and Brook left, they sat at the kitchen table until Elliot came to join them. He'd been informed when it happened that Belinda was dead, of course, but the other things he'd not known about. He said that he had a bit of money too that he wanted to add to what Allyson was getting from her grandda and father. Keegan was happy all the way around that they were taking all this so well. Now all he had to do was figure out what Andonna had done to the two of them.

~*~

Andonna held onto her grandsons tightly as she thought about what she was going to have to tell the young couple about the magic that they had received. Sadly it wasn't from her, but she was still in charge of making sure that they knew what they were getting. When her grandson squeaked, she looked down at him and could see the hint of a cry coming to his puckering lips.

"Oh, please don't cry, honey. Grannie is sorry, but I'm nervous about talking to Keegan and Kerri. I do so love the two of them." He watched her face while his brother slept. "You should be napping too, young man, instead of watching me for flaws. I'm sure that I have plenty."

They were nearly eight months old now, and she couldn't have loved them more if they were her own sons. Jasper was a good father to the two of them, and Andonna simply adored Bethy. She also loved that they were good parents to the boys.

"What do you suppose she's going to say to me when I tell her that she's marked for greatness? Hum? Do you think that she'll just say well, I am great already to move on? Or do you think she's going to knock me around a little? I fear that she might do that." William reached up for her face, and she laid her head upon his forehead. "You're just the balm I needed. Both of you are. And when you're older, grannie is going to make sure that you want for nothing."

"You do that, and I'll brain you." She looked at Bethy when she entered the room with her and the boys. "You don't have to hold them all the time, Andonna. They enjoy laying on the floor and playing around."

"I know, but I needed a bit of comfort. Why can't I spoil them?" She asked her if she wanted brats as grandchildren or nice young men. "Both?" The two of them laughed. "No, you're right. But they will have what I can give to them in the way of magic and things here. Did I tell you that the household is planning a large party for them when they turn one?

I'm sure that you'll do the same on the other realm, but for us, this will be the fae's party. What have you figured out about the house that you found here? I guess if I were to think on it, I'd remember why it was there, but I'm so happy that you and Jasper are going to live in it when here."

"Jewels told me that it was built for Jasper's father when he was alive. I hadn't any idea why I just assumed that Jasper was created like you were, but anyway, he used it when he wanted some time away from magic." Andonna said she remembered that now. "He wasn't as magical as you are, I found out. I guess I can see where that would be a problem for a man from your generation. They're used to taking over things, and he couldn't."

"No. He couldn't, and that would make him very upset all the time. I think he thought that I'd go out there and beg him to come and get me out of one situation or another. I never did. I suppose I could have stroked his ego, but I didn't have time for such nonsense. When he died, I think it was nearly a decade before it occurred to me that he was actually gone. I know that sounds terrible, but it's the truth. Even Jasper didn't miss him all that much after he was gone. He didn't like that we didn't come to him with every little thing."

"That's sad, but not for you but for him. He could have worked alongside you had he gotten his head out of his ass." They both laughed again. "I'm to understand that Keegan and Kerri are going to be here tonight. I'd like to give you a bit of advice if you'd not mind. Just give it to them all at once. Don't butter coat things because you think they'll like it better. Kerri especially. She's very strong willed and will get pissy with you if you him-haul around."

"I have noticed that about her. Keegan too. He's so quiet when he's thinking or working that I thought that he was upset with me for the longest time. But this, what I have to impart with them, I don't think it's going to make them like me all that much." She asked her what she'd done. "Nothing. I mean, I was going to just wake Kerri's fae up for her, but as soon as they bonded, it was as if the heavens opened up and rained down a great deal of magic over them. They're both extremely powerful now. Not just with magic, which is a great deal, but they have an army that belonged to Kerri's distant relative that used them during war. Apparently, they've been waiting for someone to come along and want them in service again. I don't know how they're going to feel about that."

"I don't either. However, they're Fosters, so they might just think it's an everyday occurrence for them." Bethy put William on the floor when he started fussing. "Whatever happens, I'm sure that they'll have plenty of questions for you, so I'd be prepared for that."

"I will be. Thank you." Bethy sat on the floor with the children while she thought of what she was going to have to tell the other couple. "You'll be here, won't you? You and Jasper? I'd so love to have all of them here to talk to the two of them, but they're very busy getting things set up for the Christmas dinner that they're providing. By the way, thank you for suggesting that I donate some things to it. It does make my heart feel full when I can help the Fosters for as much as they have me."

At six-thirty, both Keegan and Kerri showed up with Allyson. She was telling her about the classes she was going to be taking and how much she was enjoying being able to run in the snow this time of year. After Allyson went out to explore the rest of the realm, Andonna blurted out what she'd been able to find out about the fae in their bloodline now.

"Okay, so this man, another fae, he was powerful as well as wealthy. Why me? I mean, there had to be a time in the past where someone exhibited signs of being fae. Why did it come to Keegan and myself?" Andonna explained as best that she could about why it had come to her. "So, in all this time, no one showed any signs of being fae until I came along. I find that a little hard to believe. I mean, how many generations are we talking about? Lots, I'm assuming."

"Yes, a great many. However, what I should have explained to you, and I'm sorry, is that there were others that had the magic that was noticed. Not a great many of them but enough that it was mentioned that someone powerful would need to be born before the fae would show itself." She asked if there were deaths involved. "Yes, sadly, there was. When the magic came to them, it was much too powerful for them to receive, and it killed them. They were, I guess the best way to explain it is that they weren't the right combination of powers that would be able to withstand the pain and then the magic when it was released."

"You're saying that Keegan and I coming together when we did. We were powerful enough in our own right to take the magic into our bodies and deal with it. I'm not all that special. I know that Keegan is the brother of the king, so I'm assuming that had a great deal to do with him being able to withstand it. But me? I don't see it." Andonna explained as best as she could. "You're saying that all that, including me being a lion, was the most important part of the magic coming to us. Still. I don't know why me."

"I get it." Andonna was thankful for Keegan speaking up. "As the king's brother, I got a great deal of magic from him. On top of the other magical beings that are in our family. Witchcraft, the things that the others can do. We were already prepared, so to speak, on being able to take on more magic. And when it hit us, our bodies just took it like it was, for lack of a better term, like it was an everyday occurrence for us. To be hyped up with more magic."

They both seemed to get it then. As the questions began to be asked, she was glad that Bethy had warned her about how they'd come at her with them. Andonna was about as prepared as she could have been and was glad when she handed them the paperwork that she'd found when she found the relative. Talking them into staying for dinner, she enjoyed herself enormously and even when Jasper came over to join them, she included him in some of the questions and answers. All in all, it was a good meeting. But Kerri did tell her that she might well have more questions in the coming years.

"I'm all right with that too, my dear." Kerri then asked how they were related if they were. "We are. You're my cousin. Too many back now to be able to say just how many greats you are to me, but it's enough to know that I have more family out there than I had before."

After they left, Andonna went to the garden she'd put in for herself when she'd been younger. It was her place of peace. Tranquility. Also, a place where she could think about things that had been put before her. Like today. With the young couple.

Andonna thought about some of the questions that had been put before her and wished that she'd had better answers to their question about children. She simply didn't know if they could have them or not. But they would learn together. Then Keegan asked if they could share their magic with the rest of the family, and she knew that this family was going to benefit greatly by having a fae couple in their group. There were so many things that they could do to help so many people now. Andonna told them they could share or not share with whomever they wished. That made the two of them extremely happy. Her as well.

There were other things they asked that she had ready answers for. Yes, they would be marked throughout their life on things that they did and whatever happened to them. And no, other beings, mostly humans, would not be able to see the marks unless either Keegan or Kerri allowed it. They would be marked to show not only what they were as fae but that they were related to the queen of fae, no matter how far back their magic came from.

"It went well, Mother?" Jasper sat beside her, and she hugged him to her. "I'm assuming that's yes. I'm so glad for all of you. I did worry that they'd upset you in some way. But then I remembered that you're queen and don't put up with nonsense from others." They both laughed hard at his description of her.

"No. They were very nice about everything.

Overwhelmed, as you can well imagine. But they took it very well. They'll share with the others, just as you said that they would." Jasper nodded. He'd ever been one to say that he'd told you so, and she was ever so grateful for her son. "They'll need some help from you. I would say that they'll play around with their magic for a bit, then come to you or myself to see what other things they can do. Would you help them?"

"Of course, I will." He reached down and picked one of the flowers from her garden, then put it in the palm of his hand. Blowing over it, she was delighted that it turned into a butterfly, the smallest creatures that worked for her. "Thank you for being who you are, mother. No one could have done a better job than you with this world and its people. I love you."

"And I love you, my dearest heart. Forever." When he left her there to see to his children, she stayed a bit longer. She did love all creatures, but she had a special place in her heart for the Fosters. All of them.

Chapter 5

"I'm well aware that you had ninety days in which to pay off the money that you were lent, Mr. Shep. However, it's been twice that now, and we've received no payment from you at all." Keegan winked at Kerri when she came into the office with him. "I'm to inform you that Garrett construction will be taking back their work from you should we not have the payment in full today."

He was helping out Brook today with some of the late payments from work that she and her men had done this past summer. She didn't have many that didn't pay her, but the few that didn't, she would come down on them hard.

"I just don't understand why she's wanting me to pay her anyway. She did a piss poor job of it, and now I'm having to redo some of the areas again." Keegan asked him if he remembered that his building had been on the cover of not one but four magazines for best design. "Yes, well, I didn't know that she was aware of that. I did try and keep her name out of the pictures, but I guess they knew that she'd done it. It shouldn't matter, you know. She has more money than she has sense. What sort of woman owns a construction company and lets people pay her in ninety days? This is all her fault. I'm not going to pay her on principle. You can threaten me with whatever you want. We both know that she isn't going to do anything about it. Now, you don't call here again. Write it off or something for her. I'm finished with talking to you."

He then hung up. Keegan wondered what he should do now and figured that with some help with his newfound powers, he could literally take care that the man lost his beautiful building. He looked over at Kerri and smiled.

"I don't think I like that look." Keegan assured her that he wasn't liking what he had in mind to do.

"Oh, I'm going to like this, aren't I? What do you have planned?"

After explaining to her what the man had said and that he wasn't going to pay for the work, Kerri suggested that they call Brook to get her opinion on it. She told them that she'd met them at the building at five. No point in doing anything where Mr. Shep could see them and try to stop them. So they were going to meet Brook at the building at six when everyone was gone for the day. Keegan was as excited as he'd been about using magic on a dirtbag.

When they arrived, he was glad that Rogue was there. She was going to take pictures of what was going to happen. Also, she'd brought along an agent with her so that he could be there in the event that shit hit the fan. Oh, Keegan thought, that was what he was hoping for.

"The building can stay. However, all the improvements that were made to the outside need to be removed." Brook showed them a picture of the before of the building they were going to be working on. "Also, the parking lot needs to be reverted to what it was before. Nothing more than some concrete with huge potholes in it."

It was Kerri that figured out what to do to make it back to the original building. She simply put her hands on the picture and then sort of tossed them at the building. The building was just as much in bad shape as it had been in the picture. Even the parking lot, worse than he'd seen anything looking even in town, was reduced to what it had been before.

Removing the planted trees was the next thing that they worked on. Since there were no flowers in bloom this time of year, they removed the shrubs, planters and crockery that had been filled with large flowers during the summer months. Brook was laughing when one of her men showed up with a flatbed truck to take away the trees that had been in the parking lot.

"He's going to have a cow, you know that, don't you?" Kerri said she wished that she could be here when he came in tomorrow morning. "Yeah, I'm going to miss that as well. Hopefully, he comes in later than his employees do, and they can tell him before he gets there. I think he's going to realize that I don't play around."

"If he pays you, will you return it to the way it looks?" Brook asked him what he'd do. "Nothing.

He threatened you with nonpayment. He said that it was all your fault for allowing him ninety days to pay. I'd not do a damned thing to put it back to the way it was. Not even if he pays you upfront for doing a rework."

"I think you're right. I should have printed up a sign to put in the front of this place saying how this is what happens when you don't pay your bill." Parker showed up when he called out to her, and Brook told her what she wanted to be done. "Make it so that it can't be removed for at least ninety days. That way, the entire city will be able to understand that he's a shithead."

The sign hung on the side of the building. It was as big as a football field and brightly colored. It said, in large letters, that "Mr. Thomas Shep refused to pay his bill, and this was what happened." They were all having a good time at Shep's expense, wondering what he was going to say when he came to work the next morning.

His phone was ringing the next morning at two minutes after nine. Keegan had been up for a while, making breakfast for himself and the girls and laughed when he saw that it was Brook on the line.

Putting her call on speaker, he told her where he was and who was with him.

"Mr. Shep called me just about ten minutes ago. I didn't answer the first time he called at seven-thirty as I wasn't in the office yet. Holy shit, he's pissed." Keegan asked her what he was saying. "That I embarrassed him with the sign and that I had one hour to get it taken down. I explained to him that he had forced my hand in this as he wouldn't pay his bill. Then I went on to tell him what he'd said to you. He told me that he had a check there for me to pick up and that you'd lied to me about him not wanting to pay. I played him a little of the recorded conversation when he said that. I love that we record everything when a customer calls in. Also, and this is way too funny for me, I've had three companies pay me directly this morning even though they have a few weeks left on their net ninety. This is the best way ever to treat deadbeats."

"I agree. Now, what is going to happen?" She told him what she'd told Shep. "I can go by there and pick it up for you should you wish. I'm going to be in that general area around noon. I have a meeting with two more of your late payments."

"No, I don't have anyone late now. Thanks to you guys. The other three billings that I wanted you to call on today paid me this morning. Word got around fast, it looks like. Thank you for this. It made my day." He told her that he'd had entirely too much fun helping her, so it was all good. "Ronan was jealous that he'd not been the one to think of it. Also, he and I drove out there early this morning so that he could see the damage that we did. He loves it."

"I do as well." Brook told him that Shep was calling her back, and he disconnected the call. "I'm wondering what is going to happen with him now. Did she say that she wasn't going to replace anything? I know we talked about it, but I don't know if she's actually going to do it."

"Look. This is on social media and the news." Allyson showed them her tablet, where there was a news crew in front of the Shep building. The sign was very prominent in the background, and Keegan had her turn it up so that they could hear. Christ, this was getting better and better all the time.

"In talking with Mr. Shep this morning about his note left on his building, he told this reporter that it was a misunderstanding between himself and Garrett Construction. Asking him for the reason that he'd not paid his bill, he said that Mrs. Foster of Garrett Construction was trying to make a point that was, in his words, lost on him." The reporter put her finger to her ear and smiled. "As it so happens, I have Mrs. Foster on the line with me now, and she is playing me a recording of the conversation that Mr. Shep had with her accountant. We'll play that now."

Keegan had to sit on the floor. He was laughing so hard. It wasn't the conversation that he was laughing at but seeing Mr. Shep running up behind the reporter and telling her to go away. The man had to be in his early forties, but he looked like a man twice his age and carrying around a great deal of extra weight. To see him running was like watching a child that had just learned to walk trying to run. He didn't think he'd ever be able to look at the man without thinking of him out of breath and waving his arms to get the camera crews to stop filming.

"This can't help his business." That was when Keegan realized that he had no idea what was done at the building they'd helped with last night. Asking Kerri, he was glad to see her humor about this just as wild as his was. "He's a bill collector."

That was all it took for him to have to lie on the floor before he could hurt himself while laughing. A bill collector who thought it was all right not to pay his own bills was just too much for him. Keegan's ribs hurt, and he thought perhaps he had pulled something in his chest. When Brook and Ronan showed up, he was still lying on the floor with his hands holding his chest together so he'd not break a rib or two.

He was feeling a little better after a little while. Occasionally he'd burst out laughing, but all in all, he was in more control than he'd been earlier. Right up until Ronan asked what the man did for a living. It was enough to send him over the edge again. Keegan was glad that his brother joined him on the floor while laughing. The two of them hadn't had this much fun in a long time.

Leaving for work made him sober up quickly enough. It had turned bitterly cold overnight, and he was happy for the crispness in the air. After getting into his building to work, he found that the women that worked for him now were already at the phones. Rachel handed him a stack of phone messages as she was still on the phone with someone.

They were all from Mr. Shep. He wanted him to come to remove the sign as he'd had several companies turn him down on taking it down for him. Threatening with a lawsuit, he claimed that he'd paid the bill in full several months ago and that he was going to sue Brook. Each of the notes were more of the same thing but a little more threatening. Rachel came into his office with another phone message.

"I've sent the alpha to his business to have a little talk with him." Keegan thanked her. "You're welcome though I don't think it will do any good. He's hell bent on making you aware of how pissed off he is with Brook. I thought about sending her there, but I'm reasonably sure that she'll kill him, and that will be the end of it. Also, I've been informed that he's lost a great deal of business over this. A bill collector who doesn't pay his own bills is untrustworthy. I couldn't agree more."

"Did you see the morning news about this?" She smiled and asked him if he'd seen the world news about this. "It's gone around the world? No wonder he's pissed off. I can't stop laughing about what we saw this morning. I don't even want to think about what they're saying about him around the world."

"He's being made to look like the ass he is. During an interview with a reporter on the other news stations, he tried to make it sound as if he'd been the one wronged. He blamed it on Brook being a woman as to why he'd not been paying his bills. As you can imagine, that didn't go over well. There are women's groups all over the world protesting his place." Keegan laughed with Rachel. "I'm here until noon, then my sister is going to be coming in. I've already warned her about what was going on. She's ready to take the man on when he calls back here. I think he's going to be out of business soon."

"I agree with you on that." He worked until past noon. When Carol came into his office asking him if he needed anything from her, he asked how the phone calls were going. "Has he been calling a great deal?"

"Not even a peep. Harvard told me that when the wolves showed up there, he was being escorted off the property. I hadn't any idea that he wasn't paying his business taxes nor his loan on the building." Keegan asked her how she figured that out. "Oh, Rogue called me to ask about the calls, then told me what she'd been able to find out. You know what I think is really funny? No one is asking how the building was taken back to its original building overnight. Everyone is more focused on the fact that Mr. Shep is getting his comeuppance. Humans are weird if you ask me."

The rest of the afternoon, into time for him to leave, he worked on the charities that the family was involved in. Twice he heard from Kerri about things going on at home, and once, he heard from Loman about something that he needed to go away.

"I'm taking shots outside the country right now and wondered if you heard back from Allen Benson." He asked his brother to remind him who that was. *"He's the man that is going to have a gallery showing of my work. I've decided against it. I've heard from someone that he pockets most of the money when he has a showing."*

"I've not heard from him, but I can certainly give him a call and find out what's going on for you." He told him he'd appreciate that. *"All right. I'll do it now. Just so we're on the same page here, is the source you heard from reliable?"*

"It was Sarah. She told me that he tries to ruin me and that I shouldn't give him even one picture to hang in

his bathroom." That was a good source as Sarah was able to see into the future bits and pieces of things. *"I've been leaving him messages over the last several days. When he calls me back, he's still talking about the pictures that I need to get to him soon as the show has been organized. It's like he's ignoring the fact that I'm not going to be in the showing."*

"I'll talk to him." Loman said that he owed him. *"Nah, you just make sure that you're safe while you're out there, and it'll be fine. Do you want me to contact you when I talk to him?"*

"No. just make sure that he understands that I've not signed the contract he sent me and that I won't be working with him now or in the future." As soon as the connection between them was closed, he picked up the phone to call the other man. He answered on the first ring. Which surprised him since Loman hadn't been able to get him to talk to him personally.

~*~

Allen wished that he'd screened this call when he answered. Mr. Foster was telling him what he didn't want to hear. Not that he thought that the man was right about his brother dropping out of the gallery showing, but he knew when to talk and when to shut up about such matters.

"I have the contract right here." He thought he said his name was Keegan and asked him if it had been signed. "It's a verbal agreement that your brother and I have. He'll be bringing me photos, and you'll be holding the bag on this."

Allen didn't know what that meant even to his own ears, and it bothered him that the man was laughing. While he didn't mind a good joke when it was about someone else, he couldn't stand the fact that this man was laughing at him.

"Where is that brother of yours? I have a good mind to call him up right now and tell him how you're treating me. This is a good gallery, and I won't allow him to back out of a good thing for the two of us." Allen waved his daughter off. He hated that she came into the office without so much as a knock. Keegan was talking, and he realized that he had missed some of what he'd said. "What is it you're going on about?"

"I said that my brother has been trying to reach you for the last several weeks. Then when he leaves you a message, you call back at an ungodly hour and talk about how the show is going to be fantastic. You should go ahead and call him. He can tell you the same thing that—"

Andi reached over his phone and put it on speaker. Christ, there were times when he hated her. Like right now. She was talking to Keegan like she'd been speaking to him all along. Keegan, or whatever his name was, told Andi that his brother wasn't going to be in the show.

"I can understand your hesitation, Mr. Foster. But we have spent a great deal of money advertising this showing for him. The least he could do is give us a good reason for not showing." Keegan told her that he'd found out from a good source that her father was skimming the sales for his own. Andi looked at her father. "I'm assuming that you have proof of this?"

"I do. Even if I didn't, it's not going to generate you much in the way of patrons out there when they hear it too. According to the things that I've heard, he plans on ruining my brother by making sure that it's a terrible showing. You should ask him, Ms. Allen, about how much he's spent on advertising for the show. I've been looking through all art and gallery magazines that I can think about, and there is not one mention of Loman's show coming up. Anywhere."

"I see." Andi asked Keegan if she could call him back. "I have to speak to my father about this. If what you say is true, and knowing my father the way that I do, I don't doubt you, I'd say that your brother is right for pulling out. I'll give you a call back when I have more information to give you."

When the call was disconnected, he asked Andi why she'd said those things about him. She told him that they were true and that Loman was right in saying no.

"How the hell do you know what I've done or not?" She told him that the checking account was overdrawn by thousands of dollars and that she came here to talk to him about it. "So? Why do you think that I'm pushing to have this showing so badly? You just ruined it all. Now I don't know that I'm going to be meeting payroll on time."

"But you will, father. I found your banking information and took care that everyone gets paid." Allen told her to put his money back. "I won't. And so you know, mother knows too. She's on her way in here now."

"You told your mother? Why would you do

that to me? I'm your daddy, darling, and now you're going to be making trouble for me. Tell her that you were joking." Andi just sat there, and he heard his wife when she got off the elevator. "See that you take care of this, Andi. I won't have you ruining me when your mother thinks so highly of me."

"Highly of you? Not on your life, you big overgrown moron. Christ, when I think about the things that I've had to do to keep this family in a home, all I want to do is hire someone to take you out." Meggie kissed Andi on the head, thanking her for giving her the information. Then she started on him again. "Allen, we've been married for fifty-one years, and you've not changed one bit. My father built this place up from having showings in his own home. And now look what you've done to it. We're reduced to having clients, good men and women that are trying to make a living out of their art, leave us even before you've gotten around to taking all their money."

"It's just a little misunderstanding, Meggie. I would never take all their money." He had hoped that she'd not notice that he'd said not *all* of their money. But Andi did. She pointed it out to her mom.

"Damn it. Why are you two even here today? I have things going on, and I want you two to get out of my office and leave me to my work."

"It *was* your office, Allen. Now it's mine and Andi's. We're taking over." Allen told her that she couldn't do that. "Of course, I can. And I am. Here is a copy of the paperwork that you signed before we were married. I'm divorcing you."

A thick file landed on the desk just as four men in security shirts came into his office. When they asked him how he wanted to be escorted out, he just stared at them. What the hell was going on with his wife and daughter today? There was no way that they could simply push him out of his job, one that he'd been doing for decades without any kind of trouble.

Once he was out on the sidewalk, having been dragged to the elevator and then out of it. They had even dragged him through the lobby and out of the door before releasing him. He tried to get back into the building only to be told that if he entered again, he'd be arrested. Christ, this was a nightmare. He had things in his office that were stashed for him. Then he saw his other daughter coming toward him.

"Lindsley, your mother just tossed me out of the building like I've not been working there for most of my life." Lindsley just stared at him. "You have to get me inside. They're going to mess things up for the business, and what would your grandda say about that? He'd be livid. That's what he'd be. Get me inside, and I'll make sure that you have a job working with me for the rest of your life."

"How much will you pay me?" He asked her what she was talking about. "How much will you pay me for working for you for the rest of my life? I think that's a good question. Since you've never paid me for working for you when I was a child. How much, dad?"

"I've not thought about paying you at all. The business is heavily in debt, and people are already leaving because they found out that your mother is going to be in charge." She just stared at him. "What is wrong with you? You're acting like this isn't any of your problem. Well, it is. Who will pay your rent for you when I'm not working? Who is going to be able to get you the best gifts when Christmas rolls around? It's always me."

"First of all, I know that mom is divorcing

you. I'm the one that talked her into it. Secondly, the business isn't in heavy debt because Andi found out where you were stashing money and took it all back so that the business could come out on top. Thirdly, and this one is one I think you should think on really hard, Dad, you're a thief. Not only that, but you're an asshole that hasn't paid any mind to any of us since you've been sponging off the gallery." Allen told her that she was ungrateful. "I've been paying my own house payment for the last five years. I own my own car. Have adult credit cards as well as I haven't gotten anything from you for Christmas or my birthday in the last ten years. Andi either, for that matter."

"That would be your mother's fault. She never told me the dates or reminded me to send them to you." She pointed out that Christmas was the exact same time it was every year, December twenty-fifth. "I know when that is. I meant your birthday."

Lindsley reached for the door handle, and he moved closer to her to get in. Instead of opening the door for herself so that he could sneak in, she told him to back off. He couldn't believe that his own flesh and blood was treating him like this and told her that.

"Is there anything else, dad? I mean, do you have anything else to tell me before I have you arrested for trespassing?" He told her that she was an ungrateful child. "To you, perhaps. But Andi and I are going to be taking care of the business with mom from now on, and you're going to be out on the streets. As it so happens, I was told to delay you until the locks were changed on the house that you used to share with mom. Also, the car that brought you to work this morning is no longer anything that you're going to be able to use."

Allen was still standing there when he realized that his daughter had gone into the building without him. He couldn't understand why they were all of a sudden treating him like this. Then he thought about the things that his wife and daughters had said to him over the course of the last few months.

He realized then that not only had they told him that he was going to be leaving the company, but now that he thought about it, they had even given him the date that he was going to be out on his ass. Had he paid attention, he would have been able to put some cash away that he could get to so that he could ride out this shit storm that his wife was making for him. Allen knew, too, that she'd be taking him back soon.

There wasn't any way that she'd be able to run his company without him. Walking to a hotel, glad now that no one had bothered to take his company credit cards, Allen decided to splurge on the best hotel he could go to and have room service bring him the finest steaks in the land. Waiting in line at the counter to get a room for the next few weeks, he was actually giddy with the prospect of hitting the business with a huge bill right now.

"My name is Allen Benson, and I'd like a room for the new week or so." The man told him the price, and he didn't even flinch at the ungodly amount of money that it was going to cost the gallery. "I'd also like to have dinner brought up to me as soon as possible. Steak and all the trimmings. And a bottle of the best wine you can find."

The man said nothing, but then Allen wasn't paying attention to him as he was thinking about his wife's face when she got the bill. As his credit card was handed back to him, he smiled at the clerk. Telling him to have a nice day.

"I'm sorry, sir, but your card has been denied.

Do you have another form of payment?" he pulled out the other cards that he had in his wallet, pissed off now that he'd been embarrassed. Every card in his wallet was denied. "Do you have cash?"

"No, I don't have any cash on me. Christ, just send the bill to my office." The man simply lifted his nose at him. "I don't have time for you to be messing around with me. Just charge the room and dinner to my business. You've done it before."

"I have, sir. But your wife called here and said that you're on your own. I didn't realize what she meant until your cards were denied. If you'd not mind, sir, I think that it's time that you were gone from here." He started to protest, but the man snapped his fingers, and three big men in security shirts showed up. "Now, as you've been told before, you can leave the easy way or the hard way. It's entirely up to you."

He left. Christ, what the hell was his family thinking when they took everything away from him? He was going to make them pay when he got back in business. He wasn't going to forgive them for some time, either. Damned family.

Chapter 6

Kerri didn't like shopping. She'd do a bit of it online when Allyson needed school clothing, but she rarely went to the mall. And the one in the town over from them...well, it wasn't much of anything but a hangout for teenagers, she thought. There were very few restaurants, and even those seemed to be run by teenagers. She looked down at Allyson when she tugged on her arm.

"Can we go to Columbus, Mom? There isn't anywhere that I want to go in to shop." She agreed with her and told her they had to find her grandma first. "Okay. You call her, and I'm going to stand right here with you."

Kerri reached out to Keegan's mom and told her that they weren't finding anything in the mall for Allyson and did she still want to meet them for lunch. Kerri wasn't all that good at talking to the family this way, but she was getting much better at it. Today was the first time she'd ventured out beyond their town to contact someone, and she needed to make it work for her.

"I just ran across Jane having a meltdown. While she doesn't do it often, when she does, it's a doozy." She asked her what was going on that had upset her. *"Oh my, we don't have time for us to get into all that. She's upset about money. Not because she doesn't have any. She has plenty, but it's the fact that someone beats her to paying for something or helping someone, and she has to wait on the next one. It's quite funny if you ask me. I just do it and don't let anyone tell me how to spend my money."*

"I wouldn't think that she would either. It must be the women. I know that I'm slightly afraid of them myself." Carmilla said that she was as well, and they both laughed. *"We're at the mall now. When you leave, let us know, and we'll meet you anywhere."*

She told her where they were when she asked

her. *"Allyson so wanted to have lunch out when we finished shopping. With you and Jane. We have a few things to pick up for school, but there doesn't seem to be all that much here."*

"No, there hasn't been for some time now. There has been – oh, there is Jane. Let me talk to her, and I'll let you know what time we'll meet you someplace for lunch." Telling Allyson what the plan was, she was excited. So was Kerri. *"Oh, my dear. We're coming in mass to meet you for lunch, my dears. The others are on their way to you now, and we'll converge on you at some point. Rogue is making all the plans now."*

"That's wonderful too." She said that she had hoped that she'd say that. *"Oh, it's nice to have such a large family, don't you think? I guess you're used to having everyone around, but Allyson and I are so happy to have all of you in our lives. It's never lonely, is it?"*

"No, it's not. Dull either." They both laughed. *"All right, my dears. Jane and I are leaving now. The rest of them will be there soon. I'm looking forward to this much more than I have for a while. Thank you two for suggesting it."*

They were to wait for them in front of one of the anchor stores, and then they'd be on their way to lunch. Kerri hadn't realized that it was getting late and told Allyson that they had better contact, Keegan, to let him know what was going on.

"I've been talking to him already. He told us to have a wonderful time. He also said that I could call him dad if I wanted. I asked him, but he didn't say I had to." Kerri asked what he'd said about that. "He said it would be his honor to be called dad. He also told me that he'd never treat me any differently than he would as a child of his own because I was his. I believe him. I've seen them all around Bethy's kids. Did you know that they weren't Jaspers?"

"I didn't." She wondered how much more her daughter knew than her. A great deal, apparently. "What would you think of having a little brother or sister? I mean, you're old enough now that you'd be able to help out with him or her."

"Mom. Have you seen this family and the way they take care of each other? There is no way that I'm going to be able to help you with a baby with all of them around. Unless I lock myself in my room with it." She grinned at her. "Mom, I'd love nothing more than to have a little brother. A sister would be all right, but I'd rather have a little brother."

They talked about it all the way to the restaurant about having a little one in the house. She and Keegan had talked about it as well. Kerri was finding out all sorts of things about being mated to a cat. One of them frightened her a little. They rarely had just a single birth. She didn't know what she'd do if she had a litter of cats one day.

Lunch was perfect. They were all seated at a round table with enough room to be able to talk and eat. The place was decorated with holiday cheer, and it was fun trying some of the things that were specialized for the season on the menu. Allyson didn't care for warm apple cider. Kerri loved the cinnamon toasted coconut tea.

They ordered all kinds of things that they'd never tried before. A couple of them were too spicy for Allyson, but she was willing to try anything that was put in front of her. Kerri had never been that brave growing up, and she was so happy to see that her daughter wasn't squeamish about such things.

"Dad told me that you can't just say that you don't like something unless you give it a good try. I didn't know what that meant until he told me. It means I can not like things for texture, taste or spiciness, but you can't just hate it simply because it looks weird or smells funny. It might be the best thing in the world once you give it a chance." Jane asked her how she liked calling her great-grandson dad. "I love him. He's a great man, and I really do love his family too. All of you. You're the best family a person could ask for."

Kerri had never been more proud of anyone than she was of her daughter right then. No one, as usual, didn't talk about anything related to business when they were eating. And since they were having fun, Kerri was happy that no one brought anything up too stressful after they were done, either. As they loaded up in their cars, Carmilla and Jane rode with her and Allyson. There wasn't any lag in conversation all the way into the shopping centers in Columbus, either.

The first place they stopped at was a store that dealt only in backpacks. Nothing else, not even lunch bags but backpacks. Since Allyson needed one badly, they spent an hour in the store looking for the perfect one. Kerri hadn't thought of not getting one that the other classmates had already. She would have just grabbed the first one and been on her way. Smiling to herself, Kerri thought that her daughter was right in getting whatever she wanted for school.

The next two shops were summer clothing. Kerri bought a nice outfit for Allyson to wear in the spring and herself a couple of pairs of shorts. She was thrilled beyond words that Keegan told her that she'd never gain any weight but only when breeding. She sort of liked that word when carrying her kittens.

Stopping at the candy shop was next. She hadn't meant to get anything but the more she walked around, the more she wanted. Ending up with five little bags of different candies, she laughed when she saw that Camilla and Jane were arguing over what color mints to get.

"There are five thousand different candies in here, and you're getting mints? What if Allyson or one of the other grandchildren comes over and wants a piece of candy? You guys going to whip out the mints and ask them what color they want? I'm reasonably sure that they're going to turn their noses up at that. Especially when they hear you got them at a candy shop, and this is what you picked out for them." Jane laughed, put down the tongs for the mints and started doing some real candy shopping.

She looked at Camilla. "You going to take the mints home?"

"Yes. But I was just thinking that you're much nicer about getting me to think about what I'm doing than the others are. I like that about you." Kerri thanked her. "Also, you should know that I'm going to buy a great deal of candy, and I don't want to hear a single word about me not allowing the kids to have any. And if asked, I'm going to put the blame squarely in your corner."

Kerri was all right with that and told her so. "Also, my favorite candy is anything to do with dark chocolate. Allyson, however, doesn't care for the bitterness but loves caramel." She told her what Keegan liked. "Good to know. I don't know that I'd like that. Peppermint with chocolate, but I'll get him some. You like gummies. Right?"

They spent a good two hours in the shop after that. Kerri had so many different kinds of candy that she was sure she'd be sick when she started eating it. The others purchased as much, if not more, than she had when they finally made their way up to the register. She couldn't believe it when the amount totaled just shy of two hundred dollars.

Kerri was exhausted when they finally got home. Allyson had been dozing in the back seat with Carmilla, and she and Jane talked about the holiday coming up in a couple of days as she drove. The roads were sort of scary driving, so paying attention was something that she was working hard on doing.

"You're very nervous, aren't you?" Kerri explained to her that she didn't have a lot of experience driving in icy weather. "I never drove in the winter months. I'd have to call someone from the store. This was before there was a service to bring you your things to get food delivered. My goodness, it was terrible for someone my age to get out and about sometimes. Even now, having someone come to the house to bring you your orders is a bit on the scary side. I'm a lioness, so I'm not as terrified as I think elderly humans are that have no recourse but to take what is given to them."

"Mrs. Crumpet, you know her? She was telling me when we were at the library the other day that she'd had an order delivered from one of the restaurants, a treat she called it for herself when it was all wrong. And when she asked the young woman to make it right, she tossed her food on the stoop and then stomped all over it." Jane asked me what had happened. "Nothing. She was too ashamed to say anything more about it. As you said, she was an elderly human, and it had soured her on getting a meal for a treat delivered to her again. I asked her to call me when she wanted a treat and that I'd pick both of us up one, and we'd have a treat together. I hate that she wouldn't allow me to talk to the manager. It bothers me too that the woman is still out there more than likely doing the same thing to others because people, humans mostly, are afraid someone will harm them."

"Now that's just sad. I think I'll make a call to her tomorrow to see if she'd like to have lunch with me at the place." Kerri told her which place it was. "Oh my, this might even be better than I thought. You know that man that caught you stealing his nasty food from the dumpster? He owns the restaurant too. This is going to be fun."

It was nearly ten when they finally arrived home. Carmilla and Jane went to their own home, and Keegan came out to get Allyson and carried her up to bed. She told him that they could bring in the bags in the morning as she was exhausted.

Almost as soon as her head hit the pillow, she was out. Who knew that shopping could take so much out of a person. She didn't even wake up when Keegan joined her in the bed.

~*~

"Mr. Foster, my name is Meggie Benson. I'm calling on behalf of the gallery that your brother had declined to show in." Keegan braced himself for whatever they were going to say to him, something along the fact that they were going to sue Loman or something. "My soon-to-be ex-husband is no longer in charge of the gallery. I wanted to extend my apologies to you and your family about the way things were going with him. I will be honest in telling you that I had no idea this was going on until my daughters figured it out. All the money that had been taken from other artists has been returned to them. Allen was shuffling the money to different accounts, and we've only just found it."

"I'm sorry to hear about that. I'm also glad that you and your daughters were able to return the money to those that deserved it." She thanked him. "My brother is out of the country for a few more days, Ms. Benson. Is there anything else that I can do for you?"

"Yes. We're closing the gallery for a month to do some much needed renovations. In that time, the building will get an upgrade as well as a name change. My father and his father before him ran this place as Montgomery Gallery, and it'll go back to the original name at that time. I would like to offer your brother a deal in that he'll be the premier artist at the grand opening. To ensure that he has a good showing, not that I don't think people will be lined up to take advantage of seeing and buying his work, but my daughters and I will not only spend a great deal on the advertising, with his approval, but we won't take our usual percentage on his sales. I'd like to be able to make it up to not just him but a great many other artists that have been screwed over by Allen."

"I'm new to this for my brother. Usually, one of the others reads over the contracts that he gets. But what sort of percentage do you usually take, and what would you take from his sales." She explained to him what they'd do for him. "You'll take less than two percent of your usual ten? That's quite a discount, Ms. Benson. Are you sure that's a good idea?"

"Yes. It's the best idea that I think has come out of here in a very long time. We're a good company, or we used to be. And in order to get back on track with getting our name out there as an honest gallery, we've decided that we're going to have to cut corners a little now in order to see the big picture later down the line. I think, the three of us, think that this is the best way to generate more clients and get our reputation back on track."

"You understand that I can't make that decision for my brother, right?" She said that she knew that and that she would answer any questions that he had when he returned. "I'll give him all this information and get back to you. In the meantime, I'm going to look into things on this end about your husband."

"We've been investigating things from here, but I'd appreciate all the help we can get. As I said, we didn't know any of this was going on until recently. Of course, we had to wait to find the money before tossing him out on his butt. I fear that the more we look into things, the more we're going to find out about him that is underhanded." Keegan told her how sorry he was that this was going on with her family business. "I am as well. I never would have thought that he'd do something like this to my family's business. My daughters, Andi and Lindsley, are going to help me run it until I can get it back on its feet. It's sad to think how hard my family worked to get this established. Why my grandda used to rent out school gymnasiums to show artist work when he was trying to make a name for himself. Even times when he'd have a showing in our house for people."

"Sounds like a resolute man. I wish I could have met him." She said that he would have been shocked at her husband's antics. "I'm sure that he would have been."

After getting off the phone with her, he talked to his brother. Loman usually didn't respond to text messages or emails while he was out, but he said that he was on a break right now, and when Meggie sent over the contract that she told him about, he sent it on to Loman. He was, as Keegan had been, a little leery of all the things that she was promising him in the contract.

"I'll give the information that I have to Rogue. I'm sure that with her contacts, she can find out more than the Benson's can." Loman agreed with him. "As mom used to say, when something is too good to be true, it usually is too good to be true. Anyway, how's it going out there? Have you taken the best pictures ever? You never say that, by the way. I think that you're brilliant."

"Thanks. I've been taking pictures of the vegetation for the last few hours. I have a lot of snaps of the wildlife here. It's amazing the kind of pictures I can get while just sitting still in the middle of a field. I'll have to send you one that I took last night. It was just something that I snapped when I was walking back to my hut. I love it." His phone dinged, and he pulled up the picture. "Can you see the anaconda? I swear to you, Keegan, I nearly shit myself when it was just hanging from that branch like it was waiting for a tasty meal of a lion."

"Christ, Loman, I think it would have eaten you without a problem. How big do you think that sucker is?" Loman told him it had been about thirty feet long, and he'd bet that it weighed about five hundred pounds. "You said had been. What happened to it?"

"Nothing. Sorry. But as soon as it saw me standing there, it stared at me for a good two minutes before it slipped away into the dark forest. I swear to you, Keegan, I didn't sleep a wink that night thinking that it would be back for me later." They both laughed. "But I'm going to go out and see if I can find him again. I have a feeling that he's around close to where I was walking still. I'd like to see if I can find a nest with them in it too. Might be some nice shots that I can make into a picture to sell."

They talked about a few things that were going on with his house. Loman was his neighbor, and they had made it so that they had a joining back yard. The fence was going to go up in the spring, and then they were talking about having the pool that was in his yard enlarged and heated so they could use it in the cooler weather too.

After hanging up the phone with him, Keegan called Rogue. After telling her everything that he had on the Bensons, she asked him a few questions that he actually knew the answers to. Like how much the percentage was that they'd taken from other artists, if Ms. Benson has indeed filed for divorce and the names of the daughters.

"Okay, I'm at the office right now, and I'm looking things up right now." Keegan waited as he listened to the keys she was tapping on slowed.

"Keegan, did you say her name was Meggie Montgomery Benson?"

"Yes. Why?" She asked him to hold on a moment. "Rogue, you're starting to freak me out a little. I thought that she sounded sincere in what she was telling me."

"She was. I mean, she is. There is a warrant out for the arrest of her husband that I'm assuming one of his daughters has filed. Since he was using the mail system — why do people do that — him sending money to his accounts in the Cayman Islands is mail fraud since the money wasn't legally gotten. Also, and I find this funny, I just found that he's unable to get into any of the personal accounts, for which he was arrested for attempting, as well as all locks have been changed on not just his home that he shared with his wife but the gallery as well. This lady knows her stuff, I'm thinking."

"What do you know about the rest of her family? I mean, if I'm going to talk Loman into doing this, I would like to know that they're all on the up and up." She told him what she'd been able to find out about Lindsley. "So she works for the Feds. Do you know her? I mean, I don't expect you to know all the Feds, but have you heard of her?"

"No, not yet, at any rate." He knew that in no time, Rogue would not only know everything there was to know about Lindsley Benson, but more than likely could tell him what color underwear she was wearing. "All right. Andi. That's her real name. It's not short for anything. Andi Benson is the youngest but by far the most brilliant in the family. She graduated from high school at eleven and gone to college, where she excelled in all kinds of things. She double majored in Corporate Law as well as Internet Cyber Law. Keegan, she's been working for the government for the last six years as a computer expert. I think I'd like to work with these two women."

"Why are either of them working with their mother in a gallery?" She said she didn't know, but she'd find out. "Anything about their mom? I mean, with that sort of drive, there has to be someone pushing them into it, wouldn't you think?"

"Yes. It says here that she has a law degree too. That explains why she was good at getting her husband out of the gallery and figuring out the money. Also, she has a business degree as well as a doctorate in Art. It looks like she has been working on restoring old paintings for some time now. This is one smart bunch of people here." Keegan decided to pull up what he could find about them on the internet as Rogue did her own searches.

"They're beautiful women. All three of them." They could also pass as sisters. They looked so much alike. He asked Rogue if she had anything else that she could share, and she told him that she'd get back with him. Keegan continued to scroll through the items that he could find until Kerri joined him. He showed her who he was looking at and why.

"I think I've met the mother before. Let me think." As she sat down on his lap, he held her while she was thinking. "We have to go to your mom's house soon for Christmas eve dinner. Then we're all going to go to the party house to finish with the setup. I think it's wonderful that your mom is wanting to do this on Christmas day so that people can enjoy it with their families. I remember now. She gave a speech on being able to notice the difference between fake money and real. There were other components of the speech, about credit card fraud and such. However, that one was the most interesting to me. She said that there were many ways that didn't involve a degree to not get scammed when you're in retail. I still use that today. Even though very few people actually have cash on them anymore."

"I usually do, as you know. So that I can tip the waitstaff. I don't like putting their money on the credit card as I've heard that they have to wait on it for a couple of days. That doesn't seem fair to me." She nodded, and he continued to hold her. "Honey, we should get going. I don't want to be late. If we are, Ronan will eat all the good pies before we get there. He's a pig like that."

"You all are pigs like that." He agreed with her, laughing. "All right. We should go. Allyson left with your mom earlier today so that she and the other grandkids could help out with setting things up."

Deciding to walk over to his mom's house, he was glad to see that they'd beaten Ronan. As they had already taken their gifts over for everyone and put them under the tree yesterday, he was happy to be able to just chill out in the kitchen with his mom and grandma. Keegan was surprised to find his brother Loman home and in the kitchen having a snack of three pieces of pie when he entered the heart of his mother's home.

Chapter 7

Sarah worked the line of food alongside her mate, Cass. She'd had a feeling that something was going to happen, but she just couldn't put her finger on what it was. Even reaching out to put her hands on some of the people in the room didn't make her feel any less anxious about her feelings.

"You should know that people are beginning to think that you're pissed off at them." Sarah looked at Cass and frowned. "I'm assuming this has something to do with what you were telling me about when we were home."

"Yes. Something is going to happen. I don't know if it's good or bad, but I just can't shake the feelings." He asked her if he could help her. "Yes. Can you just gently reach out and see what you can find on what people are thinking?"

He did just that. Telling her what each person was thinking as he went around the room. She was ready to tell him to stop when he paused. Sarah asked him what was going on. He told her just to give him a second, and he'd tell her. Right now, he was getting more information to see what exactly was going on.

"See the three women that are over there by the door? The ones that are just sitting there and looking around?" She nodded. "They're the Benson women. The ones that Loman and the others were talking about last night."

"Yes, they have the gallery that he's thinking about helping out. What's going on?" He asked her that if he told her would she do as he asked. "I think you know the answer to that even before you asked me. What's going on?"

"Mr. Benson is here as well. Not in the building, but he's close enough to being around that they're a little afraid to leave the building. With good reason. While they don't think that he'll hurt anyone else around, they're afraid that if they go out the door that he'll cause trouble and someone will get hurt. He's upset that they have taken away his money maker." She asked him if he knew where Allen was. "No, not yet. I don't know him well enough to know his mind. I can only assume that he's close like they fear he is. Since you won't go someplace safe, tell me what you're thinking about doing to keep this from being messy."

"I say that we go over there and talk to the women. Then we see what they want to do. We could, I suppose, take care of it right now by having Parker go and mess him up, but that won't solve their issue right now. Correct?" He said that he liked the idea of Parker taking care of him, but she was right. "I'm forever right, Cass. Haven't you figured that out by now?"

"I must have forgotten myself for a moment. All right, you head over there and see what you can find out. I'm going to go outside and see if I can feel anything there. Please be careful, love. I don't want anything to happen to you." She kissed him on the mouth and made her way to the women.

As soon as she was close enough to them, she could tell that they were indeed terrified. Not just of whatever was going on with Allen but at getting anyone in here hurt too. Sitting down with them, Sarah introduced herself to the three of them.

"Also, I have a bit of magic that I've been using since we got here today. I'm assuming that you're aware that we're all lions." Meggie introduced herself to her and her daughters, saying that she had just found that out. "Good. Do you know where Allen is? I mean, any idea where I can send my husband and the others to keep you guys safe?"

"We saw him when we first arrived. None of us had seen him in town before we left, but he must have figured on coming here to talk to Loman on his own. I don't know what he thinks he could say to him, but that's all we can think of right now." Sarah asked if they thought he was dangerous. "Only to himself, we think. But then, I never expected him to rob other people for their sales either."

"I'm going to send the others out to find him. To either have him move along or have him arrested if he's so much as spitting on the sidewalk." The three of them laughed. "Good, you've not lost your complete sense of humor. All right. Give me a second, and I'll see what I can figure out."

Sarah didn't leave them, but she did make sure that the others in the building knew what was going on. As soon as Ronan and Loman went out with Cass, she felt a good deal better about her mate going outside to take on a moron.

As soon as Ronan came back in, she thought that something had happened to Cass. Then when he joined his brothers behind the line again, she told the women that she was going to find out what had happened.

"He's been arrested. Just now." Cass sat down with her before she could go and find him. The women were concerned as to why he'd been arrested, and Cass laughed. "He was standing next to a display in town, one of the shops and decided that he was going to mess it up. I haven't any idea why he thought that was going to be a good idea, but he tore it down and kicked the broken pieces into the street. As he was just about to start the mess on fire, the police caught him in the act and took him in. Donnelly, one of the officers there, said that he'd make sure that he was in a cell until after New Year's. That's when the shop owner is planning to come back from their vacation."

"Oh, thank goodness that no one was hurt.

I've been worried about what he'd do when he got desperate." Meggie looked at her daughters. "Andi said that I should press charges against him for running us off the road on the way here."

"You should. For no other reason than to keep him out of your hair while you're here." Cass said that he'd make sure that the police talked to them before they left here today. "I'm glad that you were helpful in this. If you're hungry, there is plenty to eat. We're just waiting on the last group of officers to come in and eat with their families. Then people will begin to gather up the leftovers they want to take home, and we'll start the cleanup."

The three of them decided that they'd eat but insisted on helping them clean up. Telling them that they'd appreciate their help, they got them plates of food and sat back down. Sarah made her way to the back room to begin the clean-up back there. However, there were already a group of men and women there washing up the pans they'd used to serve.

It was well past seven when they were finishing up. Even the Benson women looked like they were having a good time in cleaning up the tables. As they were storing away the tables for another time, Loman came out of the room in the back and began taking the trash out. Meggie helped him.

"Do you suppose he's the mate to one of them?" Sarah looked up at Cass when he asked her that. "I mean, he's the last one of us to be mated, so it stands to reason they might be."

"I didn't even think of that. How do we tell? It seems to me that everyone else knew that we were mates before you did. Is there some kind of tell?" he told her that her best bet was to ask him when he came back in. "You're thinking that it's the mom?"

"No, I mean, I don't know, but if she's not, then he'll have a feeling about her, a protection feeling that will tell him that she's close to someone that he's mated to." Sarah nodded and kept an eye out for Loman and Meggie to come back in. However, if she was looking for a tell, she was disappointed when he came in by himself and walked right by the other two of them.

For the rest of the evening, she thought about things that she wanted to talk to Loman about. He was going to be staying with her and Cass until his furnace was finished being put in, and she was happy about that. As they were watching a Christmas special on the television, she just asked him if they were his mate.

"Are you thinking that I'm man enough to handle both of them?" She was embarrassed, and he continued to tease her about it. Finally, he shook his head. "I don't think so. I didn't really get all that close to either one of them, but the mom, and she's not. However, I do like them. Meggie was talking to me about the things that are going to happen at the gallery when it's closed down, and I think I'm going to help them out. It's a win-win for me and them, I think. I think too that it might be a good relationship with us and them for a while as well."

"I'm glad to hear that. I'm sort of disappointed that they're not your mate. I liked the three of them and could see that they'd fit well in our little group." He said they could still fit in. "Yes, I suppose, but having them as sisters would have been much nicer. Don't you think?"

"Yes. But as I said, I didn't get close to the daughters, so it might still be a good thing for you." She smacked him on the shoulder, and he laughed. "I've been traveling for a while to be here, so I think I'm going to go up to bed. Mom wants me to remind you guys that tomorrow morning she is coming here for breakfast. Something about you owing her bacon and eggs."

After Loman left them, she asked him what that was supposed to mean. Laughing, he told her that his mom had a bet with him. About how long the cherry pies would last from the moment they opened today. Then for him to tell her who got the last piece.

"There weren't any cherry pies left over there." Cass said that there had been eight of them, but as soon as they'd been sliced, they disappeared. "Disappeared? Or did your brothers eat them all? I can't see that many pieces of pie go so quickly."

"Ronan was responsible for three of the pies being gone. He was asked to take some of them over to the nursing home for those that couldn't get here today. There were dinners too that went with him, so that leaves five. Loman and myself took two more of them to the police station. After that, we've no idea what happened to the other three pies. The best we can figure is that people saw them being laid out and snatched them right up. I didn't get a slice of any of them."

"So what does that have to do with the bet you lost to your mom." He told her what the bet was about. "You bet your mom that you'd be able to find the other pies, and you didn't? That's why you owe her breakfast?"

"Yes. It was funny too. I kept an eye on those pies all afternoon, and I never once saw anyone take a single slice of them. There was plenty of pumpkin and apple left but nothing of the cherries." She smiled at him. "You know what happened to them, don't you?"

"I do. And you shouldn't have to cook for your mom since she cheated." Cass asked what she was talking about. "They're here. She had me bring the last two pies here before they were sliced. And I wasn't to tell anyone that we had them. Your mom wanted to win, so she had me take the pies out of the building and bring them here so that she could have, what she told me anyway was that she wanted a slice tomorrow."

"I'll be damned. My mom cheated." Sarah laughed along with Cass as he went on about how his sainted mother had cheated him out of breakfast. "What are you going to do with the pies now that you know it was a scam?"

"I'm going to have a piece. How about you?" The two of them enjoyed two slices each of the pie with ice cream. It was a great dessert, especially since she knew that it was part of a plan to get back at Cass. Tomorrow he was going to make his mom confess to what she'd done, and it was going to be funny for her to be a part of it. Who knew that Camilla had a dishonest bone in her body.

When they made their way up to their room, she thought perhaps this was the best tradition that she'd ever been a part of. Feeding families and being around them at such a time was not just fun, but it was fulfilling too. Even as she got into bed, she thought that long after this year, she was going to keep up with helping the community like this and have their own children be a part of it as well. Things like this, was what made people more willing to help others when it was needed. Yes, Sarah thought, this is what people needed to make them all feel welcome and a part of something.

~*~

Elliot thought about the coming spring and the things that he wanted to do with his great-granddaughter. When Allyson joined him in the kitchen, she sat down next to him at the table and asked him if he was all right. He nodded before answering her.

"You and I need to make a few trips before I'm too old to have any fun at it." She asked him if he was planning on dying or something. "No. What makes you think that?"

"I don't know. It just sounded like you were making an effort to be with me so that I'd remember you more after you were gone. I don't want you to die, Grandda. I'm just getting to know you, and the thought of losing you is too much. But I will take a trip with you. As many as you wish." He told her that he wanted to show her Europe. "Really? I'd love that. Mom and I used to talk about taking a trip there someday. But with you, I'm betting that you can show me things that even the people who live there wouldn't know about."

"I think you give me much too much credit, my dear. But I do think it would be fun for the two of us. Your grandma and I took your mom when she was about your age. We had such a good time. And we came back with some of the ornaments that are on your tree in there." She asked him about the ones that she thought he meant. "Yes, you got them all. Oh, the things that we did while there. Why your grandma would talk about that time there right up until she died. She said that was one place that she'd go to every year for the rest of her days. I wish we had done it now. But, I'm sure that your daddy will tell you that you have to make time for your family before it's too late. I want to do that with you. Even though we're not going to die, I want to spend that time getting to know you a good deal more before you run off and get yourself a mate of your own."

"If my mate can't see me going on a trip with you like we have forever, then he's not going to be my mate. Family like you comes first, grandda." He kissed her on the forehead. "I think we should have as much fun as we can too. Like there are things that I want to do here. Mom said that I could have a garden if I wanted. Billy, you know her. She's going to let me help her with the horses that she cares for. Also, I want to work with all of them on being the best Foster that I can be. Like they are."

"That's a good thing to aspire to, honey. The Fosters are a good group of people, and I'm proud to call them family myself." Before the others joined them in the kitchen, Allyson and Elliot had a long list of things that they wanted to do before the end of summer. He thought perhaps they were going to be too busy with the list, but Allyson told him they'd make them. It was Keegan that suggested that some of the things they wanted to do could be done while camping. He loved that idea too. "I know nothing about camping. I wonder if I were to get us one of them great big ones to travel in, you and Kerri come along with us to show us the ropes."

Kerri told him that she didn't know the first thing about camping either, so that got them looking things up on the internet. By the time they were finished eating, not only did they have a list of places that they wanted to go, but they also had a list of things they thought they'd need in a camper. One of them being large beds so that they could sleep better while traveling.

It was nearly noon when they decided that it was the perfect day to go out shopping for a camper. Keegan had looked up ratings on the ones they were thinking about getting, and by the time they made it to the dealership, they knew just what they were looking for. It was much larger than he thought it would be when they saw it in person.

"Why I think this sucker is bigger than our first house when the misses and me got married. My goodness, Kerri, look at that kitchen. Why we could fix up a five course meal in that thing and never run out of room." They didn't just look at the one camper as they were searching. Comparing notes that they'd taken on a couple more, he was about as tickled pink as he'd ever been about something when they decided to order one made for them. "You think that they'll have it ready by spring? There are a few places that I'd like to see blossom about that time of year."

"I don't see why not. We'll have to take it on a few short trips before then so that we can figure out what we want in the thing. Also, the things that I read said that we might not like it at all." Elliot thought that wasn't likely. Just standing in the thing on the lot had them all so excited that he wanted to beg someone to let him test drive the sucker there. "Remember, Elliot, when we start traveling, things are going to be smaller than they look now. It'll feel like we're stuffed in here once we're traveling a few days."

"Right now, I don't want you to rain on my trip, young man." Keegan laughed with him. "I know what you're saying. Why, I think I'd even enjoy a little tightness if I'm with my favorite people. To think that last night when I went to bed, this was just a thought. By damned if we didn't make it a reality."

They settled on the one that got the best reviews. Even while they were filling out the paperwork, the man that was filling out the paperwork told them a few suggestions too. By the time they were sitting down in one of the nicer restaurants in town, Elliot was too excited to think about anything else but the new camper they'd gotten.

"I've been looking online. I want to get one of those maps that we can mark where we're visited." He told Allyson that would be a good idea. He wanted to take pictures and keep them in an album too. "You can hook up computers in them too. I saw that in one of them that was on the lot. I think I'd like that so I can send pictures to my cousins about what we're doing and seeing."

Elliot wanted to sit here for the rest of the evening, but he could tell that the restaurant was waiting for them to leave. Leaving a huge tip when he realized that they were the last people in the place, he apologized to the young lady that had been waiting on them.

"Oh, that's all right, sir. I enjoyed your excitement. Usually, the day after Christmas, all we get is cranky people that didn't get what they wanted. However, you guys were making plans, and it was nice." He thanked her. "My grannie and I used to go camping a lot, too, before she got too ill to travel. She always made it a point to buy locally when it came to food and tried to make sure that anywhere we stopped, we'd only shop at the local stores. I think it was her way of giving back to the places we stayed."

"That's a wonderful thing to do. Yes, I think we'll do that as well." She smiled at him, and he could tell that she was slightly embarrassed. "We'll come by here when we come in to pick up the camper. We'll call ahead to make sure it's a night you're here."

"Oh, that's all right. This is my last night working here. I got a job working with a larger firm with my degree. I'm going to be a specialized buyer for the local hospital on things. It's what I've been going to college for to learn how to do the best things for what is needed to make people feel better when they're ill. But I do thank you." He nodded, and they were headed out the door when she stopped them again. This time it was advice on camping. "Don't forget to take a very nice first aid kit with you. The one that might come in the camper is good, but not for bigger emergencies. You'll need that if you're traveling a great deal. Just a thought."

The four of them talked about things that they were going to need to purchase before they would get to use the camper. The one thing that Keegan said was that they should have it ready to go all the time. That all they needed to do was to pack up some food, and they could go."

That night when he got into his bed, Elliot sat up and took the picture of his wife that sat next to the bed no matter where he laid his head. He told her about the trips they were planning as well as the things that they'd found out while shopping. Telling her about how he was going to take her with them everywhere he went so that she could enjoy the trips as well.

"Honey, I have to tell you that Allyson looks so much like you that I'm sure you're standing next to me at times. Then there is Kerri. My goodness, she sure is a beauty." He smiled when he thought of Keegan. "That man. He's so smitten with our Kerri that he can barely contain himself when he's near her. Why and he treats that little Allyson like she's the best thing since sliced apple pie. It's good seeing young people in so much love. I never seen the likes of it before. All them Fosters are like that. Only young Loman, who I like a great deal, is the odd man out right now. But you can bet that when his mate comes around, he'll be just as in love as the others."

He laid down with the picture still in his hand, just thinking about the things that he'd have to tell her. Elliot did tell her that he was going to make sure that Allyson had her old gear for camping. Even her granny's fishing pole was around someplace. He hadn't thought of fishing in a long while and thought he'd like to do that pastime with Keegan.

"Honey, I don't rightly know when I'll be joining you, but I promise to make every day I have here on this earth count, just like you told me to do when you were passing." She had made him promise a few things before she'd died, and he was going to do them now that he wasn't in a funk all the time. "I'm going to have them bury me with that album, too, when I come to you. That way, I can show you each and every one of them, and we can think on them. I can't thank you enough, love, for making me stay around and not following you like I wanted. I miss you, darling. Every single day, I miss you. But I'm also glad for the time that I get to spend with Kerri and Allyson."

Putting the framed picture on the side table by his bed, he finally laid back under the covers and thought of his life up until now. He knew that he'd wasted a great many years just moping around the house and wishing for death. It had nearly killed him when his son was murdered along with the young man that was Allyson's real daddy. Now here he sat, he thought, about the second chance he now had on having a good life. One with young people and family that he never thought he'd have.

"Honey, I want you to tell our son that I'll be looking to tell him some of the times we have too. His life was cut so short, and he's missing so much. But I'm going to be there for him. Make up for the things that he didn't get to do with his granddaughter and child. You tell him too that I love him so much, and I've been so proud of him on how he raised his daughter, despite having Belinda as his wife. My goodness, the things she did for money just boggles my mind."

Turning over so that he could rest, Elliot had himself a little chuckle. He could see it right behind his eyes the way that Allyson had included him in everything she'd found on the camper. The shower stall, as well as the funny flushing toilet.

When sleep finally came to him, relaxed as he'd been in a long while, he didn't let the anticipation of a camping trip, still some months away, spoil his sleep. He was going to start walking more to be in better shape for the spring. Get himself as his cat out more as well. He wanted to make sure that he could keep up with his little great-granddaughter and the other children that he was sure would be coming along. Elliot knew that it was going to be his responsibility to make sure that all the kids coming along knew about their granddaddy as well as their great grannie.

His dreams were about trips with his wife. Things that they'd done as a newly mated couple that he'd not thought of in years. Elliot remembered stealing kisses when they were exploring. Taking boat rides that they never left the room to enjoy. The crates of things that he'd not thought of in years had things in them that he wanted to give Kerri.

There was the wedding dress that she's worn. The pressed flowers that she'd picked on the day that they'd met. He knew that he was smiling in his sleep at all the things that he was just now remembering. Elliot was going to start pulling things out, too, when he was able. There was no sense in leaving things packed away where no one could enjoy them when he had a family to share with. And he would too. Every last piece of it.

Elliot couldn't wait to begin his new life as a great grandda. He was going to be the best that he could be to all the kids in this family and make them his own. Yes, he thought, he was going to live his life like every day was the last. And he was going to have fun while doing it too.

Chapter 8

Stretching, Keegan realized that he'd fallen asleep. Pausing for a moment to think, he realized that he was his lion. Not only that, but he couldn't remember coming out of doors to be his lion. The blanket of snow over him made him feel uneasy. With the amount that was over him, he thought that he should have been out here for hours. Reaching out to Kerri to see if she remembered anything, he was met with a void. Not a wall as he would usually feel if she wasn't able to talk to him but an empty space where she might have been.

Telling himself that he wasn't to panic made his head hurt and his heart race. Where was he at the moment? Where was Kerri? It seemed like every question that he wanted answers to just seemed to be hanging there without one answer coming to him.

Standing up, shaking off the snow, he saw a pair of footprints. Whoever it was came to where he was then disappeared. But the scariest part was, that there weren't a lot of footprints going or coming. Like the person had appeared about five feet from him, walked to where he was, then disappeared after they walked back from him about the same amount of steps.

Reaching out to his family, all of them, he was near tears when Mom answered his call. *"Mom, is Kerri with you? I'm outside. I don't know where I am. But there are trees all around me but for where I'm at."* She asked him if he knew how he'd gotten there. *"No. Nothing. I woke up here, all alone as my lion. Someone was here, I can see the footprints, but there are only a few of them. Like whoever it was, they landed here and then left the same way. Allyson is, I have it in my head that she's with you. Correct?"*

"Yes. You and Kerri dropped her off this morning. Keegan, it's nearly three in the morning. As for the prints in the snow, who does it smell like?" Good question.

He'd not thought of that. Leaning carefully down to the prints closest to him, he could smell fae. Nothing more, just the magic of a fae. *"I want you to reach out to Jasper or his mom. They might have an idea of what is going on. The rest of us are going to wait to hear from her or you to understand where to go to help you. All right, son?"*

After contacting Andonna, Keegan was glad that she showed up where he was, and he was able to not just tell her what he'd found but to show her the footprints in the snow. When he was asked to shift back to himself, he did so without hesitation.

"I've contacted your mother just as you asked and let her know that I'm with you and that you're all right. As for where you are, you're in my realm. I've no idea how you got to this area, Keegan, but you're several hundred miles from the entrance to this place from the castle." He asked her if he could get back home. "Yes, I'll take you there. But I want to look around for a few minutes to see if I can find out who was upon you and didn't help."

"I need to find Kerri. I can't contact her at all." Andonna nodded but was looking at the prints in the snow. "Do you know who that might be? Or the reason that they were here?"

"I don't. I'm going to call Jasper to me. And a few other fae to watch over you while I search. I don't think that you're in any danger, Keegan, but I just need to make sure that nothing happens to you. I'll also have a group of my men looking for Kerri for us." He thanked her for that. "There is no reason for you to thank me for helping you. I'm just as concerned as you are as to how and why this is happening. I'm calling Thomas right now."

Thomas appeared with them in a matter of seconds. He was dressed as he thought someone from a combat zone would look. Not only did he have this beautiful armor on his body, including his neck and head, but he had a quiver of arrows and two bows on his back, along with a sword and some knives.

"This is my cousin, Thomas. I want you to protect Keegan while I search for his mate. Make sure that no one comes upon him with harm in their minds." Thomas bowed before him and told his queen that he would protect him with his life. "Thank you. If someone comes here, you call out to myself or Jasper, and we'll come back here immediately."

The two of them stood in the same place for

an hour. His mom and brothers showed up about half an hour after Andonna left him. When Thomas said that they'd found Kerri, Keegan could no longer stand up. His knees buckled, and his entire body just slid to the ground with relief.

"Is she all right?" Thomas told him that she was in the same shape that he'd been. A lioness that was in the middle of the field without any idea how she'd gotten there. She was unharmed but confused.

When she was brought to him, the two of them clung tightly to each other like they'd been apart for years rather than the couple of hours it might well have been. Being taken home by way of magic, they continued to hold each other like a lifeline. To him, Keegan thought it had been. They were both still in the dark as to how and why they'd ended up in the fae realm apart from each other.

Sitting in the living room with the fireplace roaring out heat, he and Kerri spoke about the last thing that they remembered. Thomas was still with them, of course, and his family was as well. When Andonna came to talk to them, he was worried that whatever had happened had been more problematic than it had seemed to him. She sat down on the couch to tell them all what they'd found out.

"A fae by the name of Hartley had done this to the two of you. While we might not ever know why he did it, he did tell us that it was important to him that you two didn't come together. After explaining to him that you were mates and my cousin, he attacked me." Kerri asked if he'd been killed. "Yes. Sadly. I'm going to talk to his mother and father soon. But I want you to know that the threat or whatever he'd been planning isn't a concern now."

"But it is." Kerri looked at him before continuing to talk to Andonna. "What if he'd taken our daughter? Or someone else's child? How would we have found them? Or a human family without any knowledge that they could call out to you to be found? I'm sorry, but I think that this needs to be looked into more. To find out if he's done this before and that there are people out there that are as lost as the two of us had been."

"I don't know. I don't know that anyone thought of that when we found out who it was." Andonna stood up, pacing in the large room as she continued to think out loud. "I didn't venture into his cave, where he was living, for fear of being trapped inside with him. When he attacked, coming at me with a sword, the others with me killed him so that I'd be safe. I never thought to have them look around."

After everyone left, including Andonna and Thomas, he decided that he was going to see if there were other missing people around town that Harley might have been playing with. Just as he was getting out a map, one that had been given to him from Andonna in her realm Andonna showed up again and looked visibly ill. Helping her to have a seat, he held her hand while she spoke.

"So many...the back of the cave is filled with bones. Small ones, too. Fae and faerie alike are there. Human's as well. Wings had been hung to dry. Their colors faded from the death of the wearer. Clothing, too, was there, neatly folded and stacked up. It looked as if he might well have washed them too. It was as if he was...Keegan, the bones were separated into piles. Skulls all together, bones from legs and arms in separate piles. It was a nightmare." He told her how sorry he was. "There is more. More that... he was counting the deaths on the walls of the cave. Hundreds of needless deaths for him to make a name for himself."

"Did he leave anything behind telling why he'd do such a thing? A note or something?" She nodded but didn't speak. "Andonna? Why did he do such a thing?"

"He left a diary at his parents' home that they didn't know about. One that I was only able to unearth after he'd hidden it in the walls of his room. That he was taking their magic from them by eating their flesh for it. Alive, Keegan. He was eating them whilst they were alive so that the meat was fresh and the magic stronger." She broke down, her sobs bringing Kerri into the room with them.

Keegan held onto Andonna as she sobbed about how she'd missed it. That she'd not known a thing about it. Jasper came into the room as well, telling him while Keegan was still explaining to Kerri what Andonna had found out.

"I've taken care that the cave has collapsed onto itself. There will be no more visits to the place of death so long as I'm alive. It's been destroyed, never to be spoken about again." Kerri asked if his parents were all right. "They have killed themselves rather than take responsibility for what he's done right under their noses. Everyone was blaming them. They couldn't live with the consequences of what their son was doing with their knowledge. And they did know according to the note they left behind."

It was too much, he thought. Not just that the man had been killing other creatures but that he was a cannibal about it as well. He wondered aloud if they knew any of the deceased. It was Jasper that told him that there had been a list of names in the diary of the ones that he killed.

"We were in there as well, weren't we?" Jasper didn't look as if he was going to answer Kerri. However, when he nodded, she did as well. "He didn't know that we're related. That we'd call out to you when we found ourselves in unfamiliar territory. Right?"

"Yes. He hadn't put Allyson's name in the book, but he did mention her as needing to grow up more before he tasted her. Like he was only taking a bit of her blood or something and that it was justified in some way." Keegan shivered, his blood suddenly running cold in his veins. As Jasper told them what he'd found out, Andonna sat there staring at the fireplace that he'd lit when she showed up with what she'd found. "There were so many names in the book that I despair of ever finding all the families to let them know what has happened to their loved ones. Some of the deaths are thousands of years old. Too long for me to find anyone that might well have been still looking for someone."

"How did he get away with this for so long?" Andonna looked at him when he asked the question. "I'm not blaming you, my lady. I'm only asking why no one missed the people that he took. And again, I apologize if you think that I'm blaming you. I'm not. I just want to know in the event something like this ever happens again."

"He was older than a great many people around my castle. Older even than Jasper, and he is an ancient. His magic was powerful, and he was able to hide the fact that the deaths were staining the earth." Keegan nodded. "I am blaming myself, Keegan. I should have…I'm not sure what I would have done, but I feel badly that it hadn't been found until now. My heart breaks for all those families. And for you and Kerri. What if he had succeeded in killing the two of you? I would have never figured this out without you calling to me. Your deaths would never have been figured out if not for you and Kerri."

Jasper left them only to return with his children. Handing one of the babies to his mother, she cried again. Her heart had been broken, and he hurt for her. It wasn't until she left them, taking the babies with her, that Jasper sat down and spoke freely.

"She'll blame herself for this for a very long time. I don't know what she might well have done differently, but as soon as it was figured out who it was that had kidnapped you, she went right to the source to talk to his parents." Keegan asked if there was anything he could do to help her. "Nothing to be done, I'm afraid. Nothing like this has happened before, and I think, no matter what anyone says to her, she's going to be blaming herself for some time to come. I love my mother to pieces, but there was nothing she could do about this. Not that way he had done things. If not for the diary that she found, I think that we would never have found out why he was doing this."

"I don't want to sound stupid in this, but would that have worked?" Jasper shook his head. "Then why did he have it in his head that it would? I mean, could he have been mentally challenged in some way? Perhaps something wrong with his ability to see reason?"

"I never thought of that being the issue."
Keegan asked if he could find out. "Yes. I'll have to
go into the cave once more, but—"

"No. You won't. Sarah can tell us. He touched
us, right? I mean, even if he used magic to take Keegan
and I away from our home, something is there for
her to touch and see. We can have her see what was
in his mind without ever having to enter that tomb
to find out." Keegan thought it was a brilliant idea
and called to Sarah. He was sorry when he realized
what time it was, but after explaining to her what
had happened and what they needed from her, she
was more than willing to help them.

~*~

Parker was going to help them figure out
what had been in the sick mind of the fae. His name
wouldn't be mentioned at any time. Nor would
anyone speak of the things that had happened in the
cave. His home that he lived in with his parents had
been destroyed, and a garden of beautiful flowers
had been planted in the space it had occupied. Parker
thought that was the best way to handle it and was
glad that she had been asked to take part in the magic

that had been used. However, she did worry about Andonna.

The woman had been sitting in the chair in her castle since they all arrived. Sarah thought that her magic would be stronger in the castle as it was the same realm where all the deaths had occurred. Having no idea what sort of mental break the queen might have, they all kept an eye on her the entire time they were setting up the magic.

"I'm going to drain most of the creatures around here. They'll be all right, but they might be weak for a time." Andonna nodded at Sarah. "Once I can make the connection, I'll see what I can find out about his mental well-being as well as his physical issues. If he has any."

"Yes. All right." Having had enough, Sarah walked over to Andonna and slapped her hard. Knocking her not just off her chair but also drawing blood as she did it. "What was that for?"

"Did you tell him to kill all those beings?" Andonna glared at Sarah when she asked. "Answer me, damn it. Did you tell him to do that? Did you tell him how to hide the bodies from you? How it was supposed to work for him by eating his victims? No, you didn't. Now you either get your shit together and help us, or so help me, I'm going to have Parker use her considerable magic and turn you into a toad. I'm not shitting you right now. I'm sorry that this happened, but we're no closer to finding out why than we were before because we're walking around on eggshells around you. Straighten up or else."

"You do realize that I'm the queen of Fae, do you not?" Sarah asked her if she had remembered that herself. "Yes. I'm mourning the deaths of so many."

"We all are, but instead of sitting around with our thumbs up our asses, we're trying to figure out why he'd done it. Now, shit or get off the fucking pot, Andonna and help. Or go to bed. I'm sick of seeing your sad face while the rest of us are working our asses off."

"You're very mean. Has anyone told you that before?" She said not to her face they hadn't. "Well, let me be the first to tell you. You're very mean to people."

"Are you going to help?" Andonna asked her if she had heard what she said. "Yes. You've boohooed enough. Help or shit, I don't care, but I'm not going to pamper you when you had nothing to do with any of this. And wouldn't you like to know that even if you had found out about it earlier, that there was nothing you could have prevented because he was sick in the head?"

"Yes." Andonna stood up and put out her hand to Sarah. "I give you a gift for—abusing me. I will only tell you and the others this, but you're right. I do need to know the reasons for this. What do I need to do?"

It took them a little longer than she thought it would to find a link to the man. Once they had it, Sarah had to reach out to each of them for extra strength. Parker could tell that it was draining the other woman, so when she put her hand out toward her, she grabbed her hand tightly and let her magic flow to Sarah unhindered.

"He wasn't full fae. That was why his illness had been able to go unchecked for so long." No one said a word, but Parker could tell that no one knew of him being only part fae. Sarah continued with what she was finding out. "His parents knew of what he was doing. They thought it harmless, and as it didn't come back on them, then they turned a blind eye to his killings because he wasn't bothering them. He also had it in his head that telling his parents that he was doing this for magic wasn't true. The fae just enjoyed what he was doing and didn't want to stop."

"Did he know that we were related? That Andonna is my cousin?" Parker glanced at Kerri when she asked the question. She thought it was a good one but was still startled by her wanting to know. As if there were answers to be given.

"He did know. Yes. It was the only reason that he took you at this time. He knew your uncle when he was alive the one that had the magic you now had in the beginning. His bones are there with the others in the cave. Your relative, Kerri and those of his parents are in the cave as well. He'd been waiting all this time for someone to come along that would get the magic so that he could kill the last of his line." Sarah looked at Kerri. "He didn't know about your daughter. Thankfully."

When she'd found out all she could, Sarah sat down on the floor, and Parker gave her an endless glass of juice so that she'd feel better. Sitting next to her on the floor, she simply put her hand on Sarah's and felt something that she'd not expected.

A connection to someone beyond where they were. It was a woman that she'd never met before.

"Can you find me?" Parker told the others what she was feeling. The connection to a woman that was hurting. "I'm not sure where I am. Can you find me?"

"No, don't." Parker asked Kerri what she meant. "Don't speak to her. Don't...I don't know who she is, but there is something evil about her. Something unspeakable. Don't speak to her in any way."

Parker did repeat everything that the woman said to her. Begging for her to come to her aid as she was hurt and lost. When Andonna asked her if she could bring her to the castle, she looked over at Kerri.

"Yes, but please, don't do it until I tell you. We can fashion a cage for her. Magically that you bring her to put her in so that she can't harm anyone." Parker told Kerri that she could make it so that she couldn't use her magic. "Good. That'll help. I don't know if she has any, but it's better to be safe than sorry."

Parker made the circle with salt. Then when the candles were all lit surrounding the area, she added a bit of magic to make it so that not only could she not use her magic, but she wouldn't be able to lie to them either. When things were perfect, Parker brought her to them and had her in the circle before she could finish begging still for help.

"What did you do?" No one answered her. It was frightening to see this person, this whatever she was, standing up on her own. "You didn't play fair. Why did you bring me here without coming to me? I demand that you tell me why you have done this to me?"

"What was your reasoning for wanting me to come to you?" She struggled a great deal but, in the end, had to answer her. Parker looked at Andonna when she did. "You know her? This thing?"

"I don't know. Can you...let me see what I can do to make her less herself." It took her three tries. Each time the woman screamed out in pain. When she was finally looking like a woman and less like a monster, Andonna laughed. "I do know her. Yes. She was banished centuries ago when she thought to steal away my child just after Jasper was born. I banished her to the Never Lands. My goodness, you look a little worse for wear, Alma. What have you been doing with yourself?"

"Trying to get back to you. Christ, I cannot believe that you're still queen. Even after all the things that I did to make it so you would be nothing." Alma snarled at them as she stood there. "I wish you dead. All of you for what has been done to me."

"Sucks to be you, doesn't it?" Kerri looked at her and smiled. "She is the one that planted the tumor in the fae's head. With it, she was able to guide him into the killings that he was doing so that he could get better and better with his kills until he went after us. That she had hoped would bring Andonna down, and she'd be able to restore her magic and become queen. He never knew that was why he was so ill. It was all her."

"Who do you think you are telling lies? Nothing. None of you are worth my time, and I wish you to die. All of you." Parker laughed. Alma looked around like she really expected them to just die. "Well? What are you waiting for? I said for you to die."

"You have no magic here. In fact, before I take care of you, I'm going to take the black magic that you've been using away from you." With a snap of her fingers, the creature returned to her former self and fell to the floor. "What makes you think that you'd have been able to take anything from your queen? You're not all that powerful. You do stink, but that's not really going to get you anywhere, either. So what were your plans for making anything that you've been thinking was going to work?"

"I am strong." Parker had dealt with this sort of person before. Little to no magic to be seen, but they thought that with sheer willpower that she'd get things done the way that she wanted. "You're nothing to me."

"That is true. Nothing at all to you, but you'll soon find out that I'm not one to fuck with. Other than the fact that you used black magic, that I will now take from you. It's paltry if you ask me. Why I'm thinking that you knew this all along and were hoping, stupidly, that someone would believe you and simply hand over the magic that they had." Parker stood up, reaching for the power that was hers to use. "I, Parker Foster, Grand Witch of both black and white magic, mate to Donahue Foster, brother to the king of lions, here now take all your magic away from you. You'll turn to dust as you have been using magic to enhance your body. Any and all powers that you stole from others will now go to the rightful heir of it. Magic will no longer be yours to call upon. I hereby order your death by magic."

Her screams were cut off abruptly. Even as she turned to dust, she hurled threats at her and the others. When she was nothing more than a small pile of dust on the floor, the magic that had been hers moved around the room, sweeping up the remains of the woman who dared defy her with magic were caught up in a breeze.

The magic hovered around the ceiling of the room they were in. Parker told the magic again to go to the rightful owner. But still, it lingered. Like it wanted another command to come to it.

"Then go where you will be used the best. Magic, I command you to allow your magic, now purified to white, to go to the one person that can use it the best. Without any restrictions other than what the new owner needs of you." The magic formed a heart.

Never had she seen anything like that before. The magic seemed to be thanking her for the new command. When it moved around the room again, narrowly missing the queen on her throne, it separated into two equal parts and then slammed into both Kerri and Keegan.

No one moved for about ten seconds. Then Kerri fell to the floor, her body convulsing with the magic that had come to her. Keegan, too, was hurting from the addition of new magic but he didn't seem hurt by it. As they watched the rest of the people in the room not only did Kerri get wings, but Keegan did as well. The beautiful wings of the fae.

It was only minutes before either of them seemed to recover. Once they were up and moving around, they seemed to be taking it very well. When the two of them disappeared, it was thought that they had gone home, but they returned with a large crystal in their hands, large enough that it took the two of them to carry it.

"Oh my." Parker didn't know what the crystal was other than he was large, but Andonna seemed to not just know what it was but that it belonged to her. When she touched her fingers to the stone, the magic, in waves, reached out beyond them in the room to what Parker could only guess was the entire kingdom. Whatever it was, it made the magic known to every living creature on the realm.

"I can feel it." She could, too, and told Sarah that. "It's like magic has been restored to its full strength. Like we'll never have to worry if there is enough to help others. What is that? Where did it come from?"

"It was in the back of the cave with the bodies. Stolen long ago from this kingdom so that it weakened everyone and everything." She asked Keegan how he'd known about it. "I don't know. It was just there in my mind and that I had to go and get it to return it here. Kerri and I, we both went into the fallen cave and brought it here."

Parker was home when she realized that no one had answered her about what the crystal was. She thought about it a great deal as she dealt with things and wasn't surprised to find that her own magic was stronger for it being around her. Even Don told her that he felt like his cat was stronger and larger than it had been before.

Whatever had happened, she could only hope that someday someone would explain to her not just what the stupid thing was but when the hell it had been hidden away. Snuggling up with Don, she held him to her when she was finished working on a couple of spells. They would enhance the grounds so that anything planted in it would be bountiful. Which meant more food on tables.

"Are you all right?" Parker told Don that she'd never been better. "Yeah, me, either. I hope whatever happened today is the last time that we have to deal with forces like that. However, I don't hold out much hope for it."

They both laughed. There was always something going on. She was just glad that with magic, she was able to keep as many people and family safe as she could. Until the next time, she thought. Who knew what would come their way next.

Before You Go...

HELP AN AUTHOR

write a review

THANK YOU!

Share your voice and help guide other readers to these wonderful books. Even if it's only a line or two, your reviews help readers discover the author's books so they can continue creating stories that you'll love. Log in to your favorite retailer and leave a review. Thank you.

Kathi Barton, a winner of the Pinnacle Book Achievement Award and a best-selling author on Amazon and All Romance books, lives in Nashport, Ohio, with her husband, Paul. When not creating new worlds and romance, Kathi and her husband enjoy camping and going to auctions. She can also be seen at county fairs with her husband, who is an artist and potter.

Her muse, a cross between Jimmy Stewart and Hugh Jackman, brings her stories to life for her readers in a way that has them coming back time and again for more. Her favorite genre is paranormal romance, with a great deal of spice. You can visit Kathi online and drop her an email if you'd like. She loves hearing from her fans. aaronskiss@gmail.com.

Follow Kathi on her blog: http://kathisbartonauthor.blogspot.com/